A Soldier's Devotion
Cheryl Wyatt

Steeple
Hill®

Published by Steeple Hill Books™

STEEPLE HILL BOOKS

Steeple
Hill®

Recycling programs
for this product may
not exist in your area.

ISBN-13: 978-0-373-81453-4

A SOLDIER'S DEVOTION

Printed in U.S.A.

"There must be something about you to love,"

Val said, "because I saw a throng of people in that waiting room who love you."

"Wait. You came to the hospital to see me?" Vince asked.

"Yes. Although I didn't have the guts to approach you."

That made him laugh. But his smile quickly faded as he shook his head. "Those people you saw, that's my pararescue team. They tolerate me because they have no choice. We're assigned together."

"Of course they have a choice. It goes beyond your role on the PJ team. They love you, even though you're brooding, stubborn and obstinate."

"Stubborn and obstinate? Well, now. Looks like we have something in common." His stormy eyes did a commando crawl across her face.

"Fine," he said. "It's on."

"Yes," she whispered sarcastically. "The battle of the century."

Books by Cheryl Wyatt

Love Inspired

*A Soldier's Promise
*A Soldier's Family
*Ready-Made Family
*A Soldier's Reunion
*Soldier Daddy
*A Soldier's Devotion

*Wings of Refuge

CHERYL WYATT

An RN turned stay-at-home mom and wife, Cheryl delights in the stolen moments God gives her to write action- and faith-driven romance. She stays active in her church and in her laundry room. She's convinced that having been born on a naval base on Valentine's Day destined her to write military romance. A native of San Diego, California, Cheryl currently resides in beautiful, rustic Southern Illinois, but has also enjoyed living in New Mexico and Oklahoma. Cheryl loves hearing from readers. You are invited to contact her at Cheryl@CherylWyatt.com or P.O. Box 2955, Carbondale, IL 62902-2955. Visit her on the Web at www.CherylWyatt.com and sign up for her newsletter if you'd like updates on new releases, events and other fun stuff. Hang out with her in the blogosphere at www.Scrollsquirrel.blogspot.com or on the message boards at www.SteepleHill.com.

"Remember, O Lord, how I have walked before you faithfully and with wholehearted devotion and have done what is good in your eyes."

—*Isaiah* 38:3

To the Seekers. (www.seekerville.blogspot.com)
I am thankful for your friendship and support.
My life is richer because of each of you.

To God. Thank You for pursuing us with a
stubborn, relentless love.

To agent Rachel Zurakowski and the team at
Books and Such for helping me to strive for literary
excellence. Thanks also for your career guidance
and the gazillion other things you do.

To Sarah McDaniel and Melissa Endlich and the
Steeple Hill team. From Art to Marketing and
everyone else, you do a fantastic job and it is a
tremendous honor to be able to write these books
under your logo.

Acknowledgments

Shane and Jennifer Aden for all things attorney
related. Who knew prosecutors don't work in
firms? Thankfully, you! Thanks for setting me
straight and for making my heroine's career seem
more authentic. By the way, I think I saw Pooky
sneak off with that rock-concert kilt…

Chapter One

This is the second-worst day of my life.

U.S. Air Force Pararescue Jumper Vince Reardon lay pressed to wet asphalt. Rain pelted his face.

The woman who'd seconds ago smashed her sizzling-red sedan into his chrome-and-black-lacquered motorcycle hovered in his periphery. Smoky eyes bulged with worry from a trepid face that begged him not to be mad. "I'm sorry! I'm so sorry."

"I can't look at you, or I'll erupt." Vince pushed a groan through gritted teeth and tried like mad to distract himself from blowtorch-caliber pain searing through the palms of his hands, left arm and outer left leg. "Saw you on your cell phone seconds before you hit my bike."

Correction. The custom, one-of-a-kind masterpiece on wheels that his late brother hand-built weeks before his death.

Once again the woman murmured soft words,

rested a shaky palm on Vince's shoulder. And prayed. He tried not to flinch away from her. Wanted to yell at her to leave him alone. Wanted to scream out in pain. Alone.

He clenched his eyes to shut out the pity on the strained faces of bystanders who'd come to his aid. More specifically, he wanted to shut *her* out.

But the truth was her presence and her prayers soothed. Besides, it wasn't like he could get away from her.

"Lord, help him be okay. Please don't let anything be broken."

Vince found her face and lashed a hard look at her remorseful one. "I'm not one for religion, lady." He beamed visual warning flares. Tried not to get his gaze snagged by eyes that were heavily lined and radiantly luminous. Or the stylish pixie cut that caused jagged angles of hair to hug prominent cheekbones.

Anything to distract from discomfort.

Other than desert-sand-colored swaths streaking through dark brown hair, giving her a youngish, trendy look, she smacked of "career woman." She wore sleek high-end shoes with some seriously dangerous skyscraper heels and a conservative charcoal business suit which could not camouflage her curves.

He wouldn't be so perturbed if she weren't so glaringly pretty.

French-manicured nails rested once again on his shoulder.

No ring.

And just why would he care, other than to feel scolded for noticing her curviness, if she were married? The fact that her barren finger hitched his eyes a little too long on her hand drew a second frustrated sigh.

He might be down, but he wasn't dead. The gal was stunning.

"You need to get out of the intersection. Least till the cops get here," Vince ground out.

He didn't want both of them to be in danger of getting reamed by oncoming traffic should some other driver pull her gig and forget to pay attention. He brought his hands up to carefully remove his helmet.

"I'm not leaving you," came her soft but firm reply.

She helped him take his helmet off. Turned it over, gasped then set it aside. Her bugged-wide eyes closed and her lips moved in frenzy. Something about thank you.

Against his wishes and his will, she prayed.

That it brought the slightest measure of peace angered him more than anything. He clamped his lips to keep from cursing. Sure, she'd smashed his bike, but he didn't want to disrespect a lady.

Even if she had just destroyed his most prized possession.

And ruined his chance to join his team on the type of mission that came few and far between. An allied pilot shot down and in need of rapid-reaction rescue on hostile soil.

Vince not being at the chopper when it was ready to lift could cost that pilot his life.

Shivers claimed him. Adrenaline OD. Had to be.

Once his team figured out crucial minutes too late that he wasn't coming, they would have to pull his weight plus manage their own.

Way dangerous.

Especially since they all had specific jobs they were trained to do during a rescue. There'd be no time to replace him.

Nothing rapid-reaction about him writhing here in the middle of a rain-driven road, wishing like crazy this irksome brunette hadn't been driving under the influence of distraction.

Water soaked his back, seeping cold to his bones. A rock dug into his skin below his shoulder. He tried to reposition without moving his neck.

Pain streaked across his shoulder blade. Numbness trickled down his arms and tingled fingers on his left hand. A frustrated sound scraped its way up his throat again but he clamped his lips against it. Despite the early-April cold, sweat broke out over his upper lip. He puffed out breaths but the pain didn't relent this time.

He was sure he was fine, but as a military para-medic, he knew enough to be still and quiet just the same. A killer headache was building at the base of his skull and he knew better than to move until someone slapped a C-collar on him.

"I'm so sorry. I didn't see you until too late." Words wobbled from unsteady lips. Hand remaining on his shoulder, she leaned forward, blocking rain from thrashing his face. She continued her prayers.

"You're getting soaked." *Crazy lady.* Her hair was dripping. Her expensive soft suede suit was probably ruined. She didn't act like she cared. In fact, the deceptively calm body posture he could tell she fought to maintain looked ready to crumble. Like she was nearing her breaking point.

Rain-mingled tears hovering on long lashes threatened to fall. She blinked rapidly. "Help will be here soon."

Who was she trying to convince? Him? Or herself?

And how could her voice be soothing and grating at the same time? No matter about his bones. His main concern was his bike.

"How's my ride?"

Her eyes startled open. "What?"

He clenched his teeth. She was probably some rich chick who didn't understand one stinking mutilated syllable of street lingo. "My chopper. Bike. Motorcycle. Thing with two wheels that goes down the road. How is it?"

That she didn't answer and only scanned the area around them with ever-widening eyes revved his headache through the roof of his skull.

Incensed, he released the pent-up groan.

"I am sooo sorry. The ambulance will be here soon."

The urge to laugh hit him full force from nowhere. "For me or the bike?"

A startled look stole over her face before she averted her gaze. "Both, I think. This was all my fault. I—I'll pay for it."

Again, her words made him want to laugh. "The bike? Or my hospital and ambulance bills?"

"Both. Of course, both." She looked like she could cry.

"The cycle—is it drivable?"

She bit her bottom lip until it turned white, then looked around like Refuge's traumatized mayor after last year's bridge collapse. "Um, I think not. It… It's…pretty smashed."

He tensed and wished she'd get her soft hand off his aching arm.

"How bad?" If this crazy lady broke the only tangible reminder remaining on earth of his late brother…he'd never forgive her. At her blank look, impatience mounted, twisting his shoulders into knots. "How. Bad. Is. It?" He enunciated the words like a phonics teacher with a mouthful of molten lava.

"Um…so-ome of the pieces broke off." Her face blanched the more her eyes scanned their periphery and whatever carnage littered it. "Maybe even… well, all of the little ones."

He didn't doubt that since he'd felt tiny insignificant cosmetic pieces break off on impact. That wasn't his main concern. "How's the frame?"

"B-bent. Definitely, but not horribly. I—at least I don't think so." Her lips rolled inward as if her own words daunted her. Distress mounted in her eyes and tears finally trickled down her cheeks. She blinked furiously. "I—I'm not m-much of a motorcycle person."

No kidding. For an instant, he almost felt sorrier for her than for himself.

Nah.

Her remorse probably only meant she feared he'd sue her.

Didn't matter. She shouldn't concern her pretty self with petty litigation. He'd be the last person to go near any sort of legal office. His family had a thing against lawyers. Far as Vince was concerned, they were the reason his brother...

Sirens whined closer, blared louder, derailing his train of thought, causing the throbbing in his head to expand.

Flashing emergency vehicle taillights reflected off the wet surface, giving eerie red hues to the watery seal-coat layer over asphalt smothered in oil and gasoline. Doors creaked open and slammed shut.

Several sets of black shoes hooded in blue scrub pants sloshed across the lot. Drizzle sprinkled Vince's face as the woman divorced her hand from his shoulder and leaned back, allowing EMTs to access him.

Staying as still as possible, Vince issued himself a mental reprimand for instantly missing her fruity perfume, her lullaby voice, her presence and even her prayers.

Missing her. Just—her.

Anger welled in him that a complete stranger and her connection to the God he loathed brought comfort in this momentary nightmare. He needed to let team leader Joel Montgomery know why he was late. Tell him what was going on without compromising the mission or his teammates' safety.

How to do this? What to say?

He wouldn't be telling the truth—that he'd probably just fractured or dislocated something—that's for sure. But trying to go injured could cause a new set of problems. No way would he be stupid enough to put his brothers in harm's way. Even if it meant he had to lay down his angry pride and let this mission go on without him.

He looked at the woman—the very beautiful woman—who caused all this and felt like growling at her and howling at the moon all at the same time. Absurd. Musta hit his head harder than he thought. Err, his helmet rather.

Speaking of his helmet, Vince remembered how crazy-soft her hands felt as she'd helped him off with it.

"You still got that phone on you?" Vince asked her through clenched teeth.

"Yes. Who can I call for you?" Quaking hands fumbled in the pocket of her power suit. The one that hugged a figure any guy would be nuts not to notice. Even an injured one. He jerked away his gaze like the rip cord on a screaming parachute and ground his teeth. He wanted nothing whatsoever about her to be appealing.

He'd been headed to the drop-zone facility following an emergency page from Joel. But, on impact, his cell phone had bounced across the road and broken into particles.

Frustration surged. He became even more irked that he'd been placed in the position of having to use his assailant's phone for help.

Vince refused to restrain the disapproval from his voice as he recited the number of Refuge's DZ. The guys were probably convening there prior to being flown to their insertion point.

Without him.

Not only had this bad-driving woman risked his life, she'd rendered his team one man short.

Slender fingers punched the keypad. "It's ringing." She held the phone to his ear.

"Yeah, Chance? Lemme talk to Joel." Vince huffed a breath. Ribs sore. Hurt to talk.

She must have sensed it because she moved the phone from his ear to hers. "Who am I talking to?" she asked Vince in a take-charge voice that he would have appreciated any other time.

The last thing he wanted was to feel anything remotely positive toward the enemy—who was, at the moment, namely her. And the terrorists who'd shot down the pilot he couldn't go help save.

His anger hit boiling point again. And he let her know it with a lethal look. Didn't faze or rattle her. Must be one mortar-tough chick.

"Ask for Montgomery. Tell him I'm in a fender bender and won't make the lift."

"Mr. Montgomery?" she said into the phone. "Yes, I'm here with... Excuse me a moment." She covered the mouthpiece and leaned in to Vince. "What's your name?"

"Reardon."

"I'm here with...Reardon. I—he's been in a substantial accident. On his bike, yes." She swallowed. Hard. Okay, maybe not so tough.

Vince scowled at her for giving TMI but she ignored him just like she'd disobeyed the traffic signal that caused this wreck.

"Yes, he's alert and coherent, but I think it hurts him to talk. The ambulance is on its way. Yes. Thank you. And I'm very sorry. Well, because I'm the one who caused the wreck." Her lips trembled at the words and no doubt Joel was offering soothing words to her. Traitor.

Connor Stallings, a Refuge police officer, finished taking statements from witnesses and approached. He dipped his head toward the phone. "Is that Montgomery?"

"Yes."

"Let me talk with him." Stallings took the cell she handed him then he stepped out of Vince's earshot.

Another raging hole burned through Vince. He

hated to be coddled and babied. Most of all pitied. And Stallings' face had been full of it when he'd initially rushed over to Vince upon arriving on the accident scene.

After talking with Vince's leader and saying who knows what that could further worry them needlessly, Stallings knelt beside him. Compassionate eyes rested on Vince, which ticked him off even more. Anger surged like his headache. Did everyone have to feel sorry for him?

Vince clenched his jaw at the unwanted attention. He didn't want anyone to see him weak or broken. He vehemently ignored the rubberneckers in cars and concerned bystanders in the periphery and focused on Officer Stallings.

"I guess I don't have to ask how you're doing, Sergeant Reardon."

Vince eyed one of the few men he'd met who matched his six-foot-six stature and who sometimes skydived at Refuge Drop Zone. "I've been better." He slashed a sharp look at the woman.

Although he was scraped up and in mind-blasting pain, his sense of pride and dignity were wounded above all.

Stallings' blue-silver gaze cooled as it rested on the woman. "Were you the other driver?"

"Y-yes. I was at fault." Her lips trembled.

Vince looked away, not wanting to soften toward her.

"That your car?" Stallings jotted notes.

She nodded.

"Name?"

"Val... Valentina Russo." She spelled it out in breathless syllables. Something inside Vince tried to bend in mercy.

Until he conjured images of his brother's face as he'd presented the bike to Vince on a prison-visitation weekend. The one prior to the riot that had taken his life. To make matters worse, his brother had been cleared posthumously of charges incurred by a six-man jury trial tainted by a money-hungry, truth-botching lawyer who cared more about retainer fees than ratting out false informants.

Vince hadn't been able to free his brother or save his life, but he was determined to clear his brother's name. Just as determined as his brother had been to work toward good behavior that had allowed him to do supervised shop work in order to finish the bike he'd started for Vince.

The very bike this senseless driver had just smashed to smithereens in a preventable accident.

Stallings scribbled on his clipboard then eyed the woman. "Where were you headed in such a hurry?"

"I was on my way to the courthouse near the square."

"For?"

"Court. I'm an attorney."

Chapter Two

How could a horrid day have gotten worse?

Val brushed damp hair from her eyes and drew calming breaths as paramedics lifted the man she'd injured into the waiting ambulance. "I h-hope he's going to be okay," she murmured. *And poor Aunt Elsie!*

Val glanced at her watch then at her silent phone. Why hadn't the ER doctor called back with word on Elsie's condition?

"Vince is tough, he'll survive." The officer beside her tore off a citation and handed it to her. "I'm ticketing you for disobeying a traffic signal."

Her cheeks flushed. "I understand."

How embarrassing this would be—paying the fine at the courthouse she went to on a weekly basis as a prosecutor.

But she rightfully deserved the ticket.

And at least he'd only issued her one citation.

Or not.

He'd started scribbling on his pad again.

"According to the skid marks, you weren't speeding above posted limits. But you were driving too fast for conditions, which I'm issuing you a warning for." He tore off another ticket and handed it to her.

"Thanks." Thanks? Who says thanks to a ticket? Elsie's fall and this wreck had really rattled her.

"What made you run the red light?"

"On my way to court, I received a call from the hospital that my aunt toppled down her basement stairs on a medical scooter."

Officer Stallings looked up in an abrupt motion.

"I'm new to town and unfamiliar with this intersection. I saw the light too late," Val finished, wishing her hands and voice would stop quaking. She'd never in her life been this nervous; not even in court before the most cantankerous and imposing judge.

"You were on the phone?" Stallings policed her with a harsh, discerning look.

Val stepped closer to Stallings. "I didn't want to explain my emergency in front of Mr. Reardon because I didn't want to increase his distress."

Stallings nodded but pulled out his ticket pad again. "Go on."

"I was getting information as to whether I needed to cancel court to be with my aunt. Now I can't reach her doctor."

"That's who you were talking to when you crashed?"

"Yes, the doctor. The earpiece I ordered from the local cell phone dealer isn't in yet and I dropped the phone. The call disconnected."

He wrote and handed her another ticket. "This is for talking on a cell phone while driving which, emergency or not, is illegal in Illinois."

Of course she deserved it. "I understand. I should have pulled over to talk." Val fiddled with the pewter bracelet on her wrist—a gift from Aunt Elsie.

Her sincere contriteness softened Stallings' expression. He motioned her toward two LED-flashing cruisers. "Your vehicle isn't safe to drive. A tow truck will haul it to Eagle's Nest Vehicle Repair. I'll drive you to Refuge Memorial to check on your aunt."

They got in the car and exited the scene as the ambulance left with Mr. Reardon. Val eyed the bike debris in the road as they passed. "He's understandably angry that I destroyed it. I'll pay to have it fixed." Would her car insurance cover his bike? She hadn't been paying attention and now she would pay dearly. Val wrung her hands and wished for news on Aunt Elsie.

Stallings flicked a glance her way. "You can't simply replace that bike. Vince's brother custom-built it for him. There's not another like it in the world."

"Maybe I can have his brother build him another one." The large van she was saving to buy for transporting at-risk teens around town would have to be put on hold. But such was the nature of consequence.

Stallings shook his head. "Not possible. His brother passed away in prison."

Her heart leaped to her throat. "Mr. Reardon's brother was incarcerated?"

"Yes. For a crime someone else committed."

His steely tone told her that's all he was going to say about that.

Vince's brother was wrongly convicted? Had to have been, for an officer of the law to say so with such conviction. And a detectable measure of corporate remorse.

The bottom fell out of her stomach.

Stallings steered left. "So he harbors ill regard for the legal system."

She'd suspected it when curse-laced words snaked out of Mr. Reardon to strike her the moment she'd explained she was an attorney on her way to court.

"And anyone associated with the judicial system. You, therefore, aren't on his list of favorite people."

Her phone chimed. Her aunt's doctor's name appeared on caller ID. *Thank God!*

Val cast a visual appeal toward Officer Stallings. "Excuse me. I have to take this. Hello?"

"Miss Russo, I don't have long to talk. I'm here at Refuge Memorial Trauma Care with your aunt. She needs surgery right away. Her vitals are veering toward unstable. We suspect she has internal bleeding. The only way to know where it's coming from is to open her up. Her hip is also broken. She says you're her closest next of kin and she's asking for you. How far out are you?"

Val's heart rate dipped, and then sped up. "We're on the way. I would be there by now but I've been involved in a car accident."

"I'm sorry. Are you okay?"

She fought a tremor in her voice. "I am. Please don't tell Aunt Elsie about the accident."

A remembrance of the angry red scrapes on Vince's skinned-up body and hands caused her arms to ice. Images of his badly damaged helmet swerved through her mind. And to think if he hadn't been wearing it—

Her arms went from deep-frozen to arctic-numb. She could have killed him.

"Your aunt is mildly sedated but fairly adamant about seeing you before she goes into surgery."

"Do you think she's afraid she won't come out of it?"

"I'm not sure."

"She will come out of it, right?"

The extended pause on the line constricted Val's throat. She shuddered, taking in a breath.

"We hope so. But I can't promise. With her in her eighties, any surgery is risky. The anesthesiologist is here now. At this point it's more of a risk to wait."

"Then don't. Tell her I was unavoidably detained but I'll be there when she wakes up."

Please let her wake up.

"Okay. Be careful."

Val ended the call so Elsie could get treatment. At least she was a strong believer. God would be with her and give Elsie a sustaining sense of His presence.

But what about the man called Vince? Hadn't he said he wasn't one for religion? His eyes and tone had grown belligerent the more she'd prayed. So she'd resorted to praying silently. What if he had internal bleeding, too? The sudden thought struck terror in her.

She'd made a stupid, stupid mistake today.

One that could have cost a hero his life.

Where had he been going in his military garb? Someplace important, no doubt. Or what if he'd been deployed and was just returning home to his family? She hadn't thought to ask if he wanted her to call his family.

Surely a man like that had a wife and children.

The more her mistake settled in, the more the acid reflux seared her throat. This man Reardon might never forgive her. But the bottomless pain she'd witnessed in his eyes ran deeper than the wreck today. He needed God.

"Everything okay with your aunt?" Stallings' voice crashed into her thoughts.

"They're taking her into surgery now."

Now on Verbose Street, the main one running through Refuge, Stallings began passing traffic. Probably to get her to the hospital sooner, for which she was grateful. "It might far better for you if Reardon knows about the nature of the phone call you received while driving."

"Maybe," Val said. "But that still doesn't excuse it."

Stallings didn't say anything for a few blocks.

Hospital in view, she pulled her purse into her lap. "Is there anyone else you know of who could help rebuild the bike?"

Stallings looked at her sharply. "Just his sister. But they're estranged."

"What else can you tell me?" Val asked, feeling indebted to the man whose bike she destroyed and whose life she endangered.

"If you can locate her, she builds custom bikes, too. That's an idea if you really want to replicate that bike close to how his brother built it. She may have helped his late brother design it. But it's no secret to anyone who knows Vince that he and his sister haven't gotten along since their brother's death."

She probably shouldn't wonder why. Hard to help it though. Her two options balanced on a mental justice scale. She had to do something to right this wrong.

She shifted in her seat. "Will it anger him more that he doesn't get his bike fixed the way it was, or if I contact a family member he doesn't get along with?"

Stallings made a slight coughing sound. "Not sure. Both rank equally high on the danger scale."

"Would you know how I could contact her?"

Stallings shook his head. "I'm steering clear of this one. You'll have to search that out on your own then decide whether contacting her is a risk worth taking."

"If you at least know her name, I'll obtain her contact information. I have to try."

"Don't know her first name."

"Is she still a Reardon?"

"Far as I know. You might ask Joel, Vince's team leader. He owns the DZ, Refuge Drop Zone, a sky-diving facility west of town. He's there a lot. I can't guarantee he'll know how to locate her or be free with information if he does."

Stallings looked doubtful enough for discouragement to handcuff her normally bulletproof courage and arrest her determination.

But something about Vince called to her. He seemed an imprisoned soul with tortured eyes, and it had nothing to do with the wreck today. His pain dwelled deeper than the crash, larger than the loss of his bike.

And no matter how long or hard or difficult, she was determined to get to the bottom of it—to ease the trauma life had put him through and to erase the anger that had been directed at her and everything she stood for.

Somehow, this wreck was no accident. She felt God's fingerprints all over it.

Something stirred in her soul for Vince Reardon's. As sure as the land had law, she had to get through to him.

"You don't need to be here," Vince said to Joel and the rest of the team, who hovered in a restless horde as hospital triage staff wheeled him back to the emergency room after X-rays. "You should be on the field bringing a pilot back to his family. Not here bugging me."

Why hadn't they gone?

"We aborted. Petrowski sent another team," Joel said as though perceiving his question.

"Yeah, thanks to Stallings' loose lips and a reckless-driving woman's big mouth," Vince bit out. Mostly because mentioning her mouth evoked pleasant images more than unpleasant memories of the collision she'd caused.

A paternally stern look entered team leader Joel's eyes. But so what? It was his bad day and he had a right to be rude and testy. At least outwardly. Didn't help matters that his skin burned like fire from scrapes and nurses' merciless cleaning of them. Speaking of, Nurse Torture stepped toward the door. "I need to see another patient."

"Good." Vince started to fold his arms but stopped. Pain clenched his shoulders.

He didn't want to see or talk to anyone right now and especially not the crazy lady who crashed his bike and brought a bomb of worry crashing down on his team.

Worry for nothing. "It's not like the wreck was fatal."

"No, but it could have been," Joel said.

"Well it, wasn't. So you can all go home."

His teammates eyed one another, but refused to

budge. If it wouldn't hurt his scraped-raw jaw to cuss, he would.

Aaron Petrowski, commander over three pararescue teams within their joint task force, entered the room and stood by Joel. Both were strong military leaders and two of Refuge's most well-respected men. They also had the most solid faith of anyone he knew. Not that he'd admit it to their faces.

Why couldn't his dad have been that kind of man? Then maybe his childhood wouldn't have been so humiliating. Son of the town drunk. That's what he'd been known for. And he'd grown to despise pity because of it.

Petrowski leaned over his side rail. "Saw your bike. Or what's left of it."

Vince cringed inwardly.

Manny Peña knuckled Vince's unscathed shoulder. "Boy, I think you got me beat. Word on the street is you had a world-class crash."

Vince raised the head of his bed. "Yeah, but my accident wasn't my own fault." He made sure to inject heavy doses of sarcasm in his words.

Manny grinned. Then his face sobered. "Seriously, Reardon. I'm glad you're okay." He assessed Vince's bandages. "For the most part."

Vince despised the sympathy in his stocky teammate's eyes. Or maybe it was empathy.

Manny had crashed a parachute a couple years back. The one jump in Manny's history that he'd left the plane without his hook knife. When a line-over collapsed his main chute, he couldn't cut it away. When he'd activated the reserve chute, it tangled on the malfunctioning main chute and he'd crashed into the only grove of trees for miles.

Vince's respect for Manny ramped though. The dude had to have been in much more pain than Vince was in now.

Teammate Chance moved in. "Yeah. You're blessed to be alive."

Blessed? Since *when* did Garrison start using churchy words? If one more member of his team crossed over to the dark side—as Vince deemed Christianity—he'd…well, he didn't know what he'd do. Be hard-pressed for partying buddies, that's what.

For once the thought of alcohol caused a sour taste to settle in Vince's mouth. For *sure* he'd smacked his skull.

Joel eyeballed Chance then Vince. "God protected you, bud."

It was on Vince's tongue to remark against that and say that God hadn't protected him, Vince just cheated death. But something stopped him. Weird. He never would have thought twice about spouting something like that before. If nothing other than to rile Joel.

A knowing settled deep inside. He'd felt protected by someone much bigger than himself. He couldn't deny that.

Joel was right. The wreck could have killed him. Or caused permanent brain damage or spinal-cord injuries. None of which showed up on the barrage of tests Refuge's trauma team put him through in the past hours.

Minor injuries, arm and leg abrasions from the skid and a slight concussion from impacting pavement at high speed were his only diagnoses. Doctors were calling him a miracle. Whatever. His mind would normally refute the word with vehemence.

But for some reason, this time the word sobered him.

The foreign feeling that had filtered through him back at the accident scene when the woman prayed fell in around him again. Tangible. Soothing. Like warm water on a cold day. He felt drugged. But he'd refused pain meds.

"You're skinned up pretty good," Joel observed as a doctor salved Vince's arm scrapes then bandaged them.

"Still. You should be overseas with someone *really* hurt. Ridiculous that you guys chose to stay with a bike-wreck victim over a pilot whose plane crashed."

"You're not just a bike-wreck victim, Vince. You're our brother." Ben Dillinger bumped gentle knuckles into Vince's uninjured shoulder.

"No way were we gonna leave you, not knowing how bad you were," Petrowski added.

Everything in Vince wanted to flail against the friendship that had caused his team to choose him over a mission.

But looking into the eyes of his team—Leader

Joel, Mountain Manny, Gentle Ben, Compassionate Nolan, Wise Aaron, Shy Chance and Boisterous Brock—Vince couldn't bring himself to scrutinize their decision. He'd have done the same for each of them had fate's tables been turned.

He clenched his jaw against an agitating sense of belonging. One he didn't want to grow too comfortable in. He didn't feel deserving of their love and sympathy.

If he was a soft kinda guy, their concern could get to him as far as stirring his emotions. He blinked and cleared a foreign knot from his throat. Alien emotions rushed forward and pressed against the back of his eyes. Vince clenched his jaw and blink, blink, blinked.

The guys eyed him then one another, surprise evident.

His hackles rose. "What? Hospital's dry. Makes my eyes water." He ground his teeth and wanted nothing more than to go home and sulk alone.

No one looked convinced. He scowled and huffed.

A nurse entered, breaking the moment. "Ready to get out of here?"

He yanked down his side rail and stood so fast she jumped. "I'll take that as a yes." Laughing, she brandished his instructions. "Take it easy for a few days. Doc says no skydiving or dangerous activities for a couple of weeks."

Vince opened his mouth to protest but Petrowski's hand clamping his shoulder stopped him. "We'll make sure he has desk or rigging duty until his doctor clears him."

Rigging chutes? He'd rather eat overgrown slugs. But desk duty was worse than rigging. A sitter he was not. A rigger he could be and survive. Anger resurfaced over the woman who sent his day south. Two weeks? Not only would he be at risk of death by boredom, he'd miss important training sessions with recruits. And for what? To be holed up in a back room with a bunch of parachutes that he'd have to fold instead of fly. Better than desk duty though.

He bypassed the wheelchair the nurse brought him and limped with his team toward the exit. They stayed close but knew well enough not to try and lend a hand. Speaking of, something else hit him.

He faced his superiors. "I'll still be able to launch Refuge's community swim-safety program, right?"

The cautious looks Petrowski passed Joel told Vince he probably didn't want to know the answer to that.

Once again, ire flared against the woman who caused these problems. He wrestled mental frustration at thoughts that the community programs would be delayed, therefore risking the sponsors' continued support.

Pressure-cooked anger boiled inside his lidded emotions to the point of explosion.

"If Miss Russo knows what's good for her, she'll steer completely clear of me."

Chapter Three

"How's the pilot?" Vince asked Petrowski through a door in a back room at the DZ the next week.

Chunka-chunka-chunka of a sewing machine whirred behind him. Chance, at its helm mainly to keep Vince company, paused as Petrowski stepped inside.

Vince surveyed this morning's work lining the cubbyholes on the far wall. Neon parachute harnesses and canopies hung to his left.

Sewn canopies rested on a stainless-steel work desk against the wall behind him.

"Not sure yet." Petrowski stepped over a parachute stretched across folding mats on the spacious floor.

Something in Vince's gut said Petrowski was withholding information. His prerogative, he guessed. But every day that pilot remained unfound added sobering percentage to the possibility that he wouldn't be found alive.

Joel entered. "What's making you bark this time, Reardon?"

Vince tamped down his acrid mood because he didn't want to stir the volatile pot and disrespect the authority of the man who was also his friend. "I mean no disrespect, sir, but there was no need not to send our guys to attempt that rescue last week." Vince swiped up his plastic jug and swigged his water, wishing it was a cold beer instead. Then just as fast, the thought of tasting beer turned uncharacteristically sour. Way weird.

Maybe he had some undetected brain damage from the wreck. No other rational explanation for him not wanting to down a cold one.

Chance abandoned the sewing and knelt to fold the next chute in the lineup.

Vince dropped to his knees to help. "Though I'm sure they're properly trained, they don't have as much experience with pilot rescue as we do."

Petrowski stood to his full height. "Then they needed the practice, didn't they?"

"Yeah, but—they could practice during training. This was a *real* mission with an actual human *life* at stake, sir." Frustration surged over the fact.

Joel shifted his stance. "Don't ride Petrowski, Reardon. We requested he send another team as long as it wouldn't further jeopardize the pilot."

"Fine." Vince's diamond-plate will yielded. He trusted and respected his leaders and their decisions. Period. That still didn't explain why they'd choose him over bringing a pilot back. That went completely against their creed. And against any good reason Vince could wrap his mind around.

Unless Vince meant more to them.

Nah. Not possible. Right? Not as intentionally difficult and brooding and belligerent as he strove to be.

Vince folded his arms across his chest and grunted. "I think all your sanities just fell off a corporate cliff."

But the deep care embedded in their eyes said otherwise.

Petrowski leaned in, eyeing Vince's elbow. "That has to hurt. But I expected you to look worse only a week after your wipeout." He smirked.

Now that was more like it. Let them give him grief. Give him a hard time. Give him relentless razzing. Anything was better than the pity plastered on their faces upon seeing him ride down the hall strapped helplessly to an annoyingly creaky gurney last week.

"That's because that dame who hit me blasted things out of proportion."

"Whoa, grumpy," a familiar voice said from the doorway.

Refuge's Sheriff Steele and Officer Stallings walked in with an armload of his things.

"I recovered your stuff." A metallic *clank* sounded as Stallings laid the items on an empty stainless-steel table.

Rounds of surprise rumbled through the room from each member of his team.

Obliterating silence followed as his leaders and fellow PJs eyed the objects.

Or what was left of them.

Vince swallowed hard. So did most of his team. If it hadn't been for the thick leather jacket and helmet he had worn, he would have been far worse off.

Stallings handed Vince his scuffed-up wallet. "There's a copy of the police report at the station once you feel up to filling your portion out. Although the other driver was cited for infractions, you should know she was distracted by a family emergency."

Vince blinked. What kind of family emergency? She'd said she was on her way to court. So which time was she lying? Figured. Didn't all attorneys?

"So, go easy on her," Stallings was saying. "She's fully prepared to take responsibility for the accident."

"She admitted fault?" An *attorney?*

"Yes. Without hesitation. And she was insured." Stallings' gaze veered toward the helmet and the scuffed black jacket that had shredded down to his skin.

Vince's arms tingled at the thought of how much worse he could have fared.

"You ought to thank the Big Man Upstairs that you're alive." Stallings jabbed a pointer finger toward the ceiling a couple times to drive his divine point home, then stepped out.

Silence pervaded for several moments.

Vince peered at the items. Joel walked over and lifted them up one by one. Vince's other teammates moved close to look. Vince raised his head to see over Brock's broad back and Chance's tall shoulders.

"Wow. *Dude.*"

Who said that, Vince couldn't be sure. His mind had skidded back to the moment of impact. He forced images away and focused on his rain-and-red-soaked belongings.

The bloodstained leather was mangled into shreds, the inside of the material scraped from asphalt and oil on the arms where he'd skidded.

Joel whistled long and lifted Vince's helmet.

His very scraped helmet.

"That could have been your skull, Reardon," Joel said.

What could he say to that? Certainly couldn't refute it. He'd only recently begun wearing one, ever since Stallings had pulled him over for the third time and told him it was the law.

"Lemme see that." Vince held out his hand. Joel placed the helmet in it.

Vince turned it over in his hands while his team looked on. His helmet was scraped down the back and the inner foam lining was compressed from absorbing impact.

Joel was right. That could have been his skull had he not been wearing it. In that moment Vince knew he would not be sitting here alive had he not been wearing it. And, not that he'd admit this quite yet, but maybe Someone upstairs did spare his life.

Why?

Why did God think him worth saving when good people died every day?

"Anything else there?" Vince asked, growing uncomfortable with his own thoughts.

No telling what had happened to his gloves. But they'd been a gift from his dad. One of the only things the drunken old codger had ever given him besides a hard life and a hard time. The old man spent all his money on booze.

Chance poked his head in the door and extended a cordless phone. "Petrowski, Central with word on the missing pilot."

Chance's solemn tone did not make Vince feel good. Aaron took the call in hushed words. When he peered over his shoulder, shook his head in somber motions and gestured Joel out, Vince cursed and looked around for something to punch just like the truth hitting him in the gut.

The pilot wasn't coming home. Not alive, anyway.

Vince's lingering headache expanded into something monstrous. Part of it was probably from worrying about the pilot's family and how miserable the novice PJ team must feel right now. And his own misery over his jacked-up bike. And his hopelessness over his old man who refused to stop drinking. And his ruined relationship with the sister he still loved so much it hurt. Yet both of them were too stubborn to reach out first.

No use pining for things that couldn't be fixed.

He thought of the pilot and of his brother.

Or continue to ache and seethe over someone who couldn't be brought back from wherever souls go when they die.

But knowing that didn't afford him the ability to let go. And now, some senseless woman had sabotaged a crucial mission and severed the one final connection he still felt he had with his brother.

And he didn't know if he could ever forgive her.

"I wouldn't do that if I were you."

The familiar voice paused Val at the DZ entrance. She faced the man leaving and realized he wasn't in uniform. "Officer Stallings."

"Miss Russo." He viewed the stuff in her arms. "For Vince?"

Her toe dug into the asphalt. "Ah, yeah."

"Peace offering?" His head dipped toward the items.

Val plucked at her gift. A stuffed tan bear wearing a camouflage outfit, a tiny parachute and airplane Band-Aids she'd placed on his arms. "I found it at the gift shop near the unmapped military base on the outskirts of Refuge."

She'd gone there yesterday after leaving the hospital where she'd checked on Elsie, scheduled for another surgery today.

When Val had called the police station last week to ask about Vince, the dispatcher had informed her she'd crashed into one of the town's infamous PJs. Val wasn't even from around Refuge, and had heard of them. Didn't take much sleuthing to figure out she could find Vince at the Refuge Bed and Breakfast on Mustang Lane or at the DZ near Peña's Landing.

"I went to the B and B and inquired about Vince. A nice woman named Sarah told me I could find Vince here. She offered directions to the DZ facility. So, is he in there?" She eyed the suddenly formidable-looking building.

"Yeah." He angled toward her. "I hope you're not planning to go in there with that stuff just yet."

"Why not?" Val stepped into the DZ lobby.

Stallings trailed, looking ten kinds of tense. Like he might be gearing up to referee a domestic disturbance. "He's still pretty steamed under the collar. And Vince is a hothead, anyway. That bear's liable to have its limbs torn off and you're liable to walk out wearing the stuffing."

"It's a chance I'll take unless you think my presence will compromise his recovery."

Stallings snorted. "It's not Vince's health I'd be worried about. Miss, I'm telling you, he's not one to mess with when he's this mad. I suggest you either send it in with someone else or come back at a later date. Ten years from now ought to do it."

Though vaguely amused, she grew irritated and eyed her watch. She needed to be back at the hospital soon. Elsie would be out of her second surgery anytime now if everything had gone well. Val shoved the bear toward Stallings. "Then would you mind taking it in to him?"

Stallings' eyes bugged. He backed away from the

bear. "Me? Uh, no, ma'am." He grabbed another officer coming out of a back room. "But Sheriff Steele here will."

The stubby sheriff paused. Fluorescent bulbs buzzing above reflected light off his shiny bald head as it bobbled up and down to study her and Stallings. "Why do I get the feeling I've stumbled into a speed trap?" Steele adjusted his belt which secured a sidearm peeking under his paunch.

She extended the bear toward the sheriff. "I'm in a hurry. And you're armed. So why don't you take this in to Mr. Reardon for me?" She smiled her brightest smile and hoped it carried enough charm to convince him to do it.

The sheriff tilted back his hat. "And who might you be, little lady? A love interest?"

Val coughed out a laugh.

Stallings, on his way out, paused and snorted as he left the facility through the lobby, which boasted a wall of floor-to-ceiling windows.

"N-no. Certainly not a love interest. I—" Val cleared her throat of the sudden glob of fear.

The sheriff raised snowy brows and bounced on the balls of his feet in an impatient gesture. He made an exaggerated motion of eyeing his watch. "I'm not sure I've got the time unless you've got more info. I'm friends with the stubborn cuss's old man. Jest dropped by to check on him. Who are you?"

"I'm the woman who hit him. And destroyed his bike."

A blank look. Then the sheriff looked her up and down—and laughed. His cheeks and chin jiggled as he laughed some more. Then he clamped a grandfatherly palm on her shoulder. "Tell you what, miss. I promise to take him this little bear if you'll promise not to be a stranger. Come back and visit Vince when he ain't so rip-roarin' mad."

"Um…err…okay. Why?"

A jovial twinkle lit his aged eyes. "Because once he cools down enough and gets past being so blasted mad that he can't see straight, I think he'll see that you're a mite too perty to stay mad at." He winked, tipped his hat and reached for the bear. "Any message you want me to give?"

"Just what's on the card. That I'm very sorry. And fully willing to pay for all the damages. My contact information is included."

He nodded and headed toward a partially closed room that voices wafted from. She turned, pausing as a group of massive men strode out of the room to stand in the hall near where the sheriff stepped in to talk to Vince. No yelling or things crashing. Maybe Vince was taking the bear, and her apology, okay.

"Can I help you, miss?" One of the daunting men approached. His name tag read "Peña."

"I've been helped. Thanks."

But the stocky Hispanic man didn't budge.

Curious glances hurtled her way from the imposing group of muscle-bound men who undoubtedly wondered what she was doing standing there staring at the door of a room she imagined housed Vince. Still no sound coming from inside.

She wished she had assurance Vince would be okay with her coming to his work.

"Excuse me," she said to the one whose eyes held the deepest shade of compassion and blue. His name tag read "Briggs." He seemed much less intimidating than the rest.

"Yes?" The man stepped forward.

"I'm wondering if you can tell me how Mr. Reardon is faring."

The other guys stood in the wide connecting hall opposite the table area and studied her. Then each other. Heavy silence fell. Stark. Foreboding. Like a cell block door slam. The hefty weight of all the eyes bearing down on her settled over her like a judge's declaration of life without parole.

Shades of suspicion turned Briggs's narrowing eyes into a treacherous tint of blue. "Who wants to know?"

She swallowed, feeling suddenly surrounded by dangerous men—a protective band of brothers—who had to be part of Mr. Reardon's pararescue team. No other explanation for why they'd be so physically daunting.

She refused to wilt. Her chin lifted. So did the man's. Which rattled her like a box of banging gavels. Never let them see you sweat. She applied the courtroom principle to her body language.

"I do." She straightened her shoulders but softened

her poker face and stuck out her hand, hoping he'd take it.

"And you are?" he asked as he shook her hand.

"Valentina Russo. My friends call me Val."

His eyes flashed recognition. His fingers snapped in the air. A slow grin came to his face. "The woman who crashed into his bike."

She licked parched lips. So they'd heard her name. Couldn't be good. Especially since the emphasis landed on her crashing the bike rather than Vince. "Yes."

"I'm Airman Briggs. But you can call me Nolan." Thankfully, his demeanor softened.

She nodded. "Nice to meet you."

"What can we help you with?"

"I just wanted to be sure he's okay. Understandably, the hospital wouldn't give out information when I called last week."

Nolan didn't respond.

She plucked nervously at her earring. "I haven't been able to get him off my mind."

Nolan grinned. "The bear you sent in there? Or Vince?"

Gentle humor in his eyes broke her nervousness. She loosed a laugh, which was more relief. "Vince."

Nolan nodded slowly and appeared to ponder her deeply. "How'd you know where to find him?"

"Apparently your PJ team holds celebrity status in these parts. I asked around town and was sent to the B and B. A lady named Sarah directed me here."

"Did you say Sarah?" Nolan looked at the older man on their team, who set his clipboard down and came close. His face reflected acute interest in the conversation.

"Yes. She guided me here, saying I'd probably find Vince here."

The redheaded teammate snickered. "Guided, wow. Sounds like something someone would do with an airborne missile."

Val stared at him. "I'm sure Sarah meant no harm by guide—I mean sending me here."

The older man grinned. "Relax, ma'am. Sarah's my fiancée."

Nolan smiled. "Vince is tough. He'll be all right. No permanent injury. But I think it'd be better for you both if you didn't come around him."

The man whose tag identified him as Petrowski, and who'd proudly proclaimed Sarah as his fiancée, moved to stand alongside Nolan. "Least, not right now." A slight grin smoothed rigid lines from his face.

"It's been a week since the wreck. You think he's still that angry?" Val asked.

"Now, now. Calm down, airman. I'm just the messenger," came from inside the back room. Sounded like the sheriff's voice. Only a little higher-pitched. Just then a growl gurgled from the room. The next instant the stuffed bear whizzed by her, hitting the opposite corridor wall.

Nolan grinned at her. "Apparently so. Give him

another week. At least." His face grew serious. "He really loved that bike."

Which she'd learned from Eagle's Nest's mechanic was damaged beyond repair.

Nothing is beyond repair in Your eyes, God. Not things. Not people. Help me at least give him part of his bike back.

Maybe she should follow through with contacting Vince's sister and have her try to use its salvaged parts to rebuild Vince's bike. How wide was the rift between her and Vince? Would the sister even be willing?

If so, it would likely take most of Val's savings to do this. Savings she'd been counting on to buy a van and rent a facility to entertain the at-risk youth she'd moved here to help. Oh well. She'd just have to be more creative in thinking up alternate fun activities.

Her insurance would probably cover most of the cost of a new bike, but it was doubtful that it would stretch to the custom rebuilding. If it did, the insurance company would want to choose the repairman rather than letting Val use Vince's sister. If not, she'd just have to pick another place to take teens prone to trouble. Continue the work her aunt had started then grown too ill to finish.

Not to mention she had a hard phone call to make.

Her dad would blow his bad toupee when he found out she'd wrecked the car he and Mom had bought for her when she'd passed her bar exam. A ridiculously expensive car that symbolized prestige and privilege. An image she hadn't enjoyed growing up under. He'd think she'd wrecked it on purpose. Ludicrous, but such was the way with her often eccentric and unreasonable father.

"Anything else?" Nolan's voice clashed into her thoughts.

"Maybe. I wonder if you could tell me how to reach Vince's sister."

Nolan's raised his brows. "Lady, you really do have a death wish, don't you?"

The looks on the rest of the men's faces said the same. The worst possible thing she could do was contact Vince's sister.

The stern warning in Nolan's eyes suggested doing so would be like tossing gasoline on the flame of Vince's rage.

"But that's the only hope of rebuilding his bike like his brother had it. The officer at the scene, Stallings, said she designed the bike Vince's brother hand-built."

"She did. But that was before the brother's death and subsequent rift that ripped their family apart. Trust me. You'd be better off to walk away from this altogether."

One flash of memory of the deep void of emptiness and pain in Vince's darker-than-midnight eyes as he lay on the wet asphalt, and Val knew that walking away from this was exactly opposite of what God was asking her to do.

Trust Me.

Only it wasn't Nolan but God impressing this upon her. An inner voice. Remembering the battle in Vince's face as she'd prayed. Tiny sparks of hope in the most tortured eyes she'd ever seen.

She'd looked deeper.

And God had allowed her to see.

And Vince had been too momentarily unguarded to stop her. What she'd seen was a little boy wounded by life and growing up into a hard and cold brooding man who refused to feel or even act as though he could feel. That kind of ultra self-protective pain.

She saw it in the faces of abused and neglected children she lived her life to help. And in the dullness coating the eyes of teens nearly too late to help.

And she'd seen it in Vince's eyes.

"I'm sorry. But I can't walk away. Not from this."

Chapter Four

She had some nerve.

Vince stormed from the back room. His team tensed. Petrowski stepped between him and Miss Distraction. Mass distraction rather. A weapon of mass distraction. Yeah. That's what she was.

And he wanted no part of her.

Vince didn't care why she'd come.

Only cared to see to it that she didn't come back.

He let incisive anger fly from his eyes as he surged purposefully toward her.

Fear came alive in her face, making him pause momentarily. Her expression slammed memories back of seeing his sister's face like that when their dad came crashing home in one of his drunken rages. Vince halted, unable to unleash the verbal lashing his tongue longed to give a hot moment ago.

As if sensing his sudden calm, his team inched away, except for Joel and Aaron, who no doubt hung out either from curiosity or at the risk of seeing if they'd have to step in and referee.

Vince unclenched his fists. "Why are you here?"

"I—I came to say I'm sorry."

"You already did. About seven hundred times. Doesn't change anything."

"What can I say to that?" She raised her arms loosely and let them fall hard at her side. "I just hoped it would make a difference this time."

Pure frustration. Not put on.

Honest. Tough. Vulnerable.

How she was all three at the same time, he had no idea. He just knew she was.

He notched his chin up. "What do you want from me?" He'd said it so calmly, the surprise in her eyes mirrored how he felt inside.

Thick black lashes on gorgeous gray eyes fluttered. "I—I don't— I'm not sure." Backing toward the door, she eyed the clock behind him. "I'm sorry that I came. I didn't mean to make matters worse." She turned and fled as fast as her high heels would take her.

She looked back only once. Regret sliced through him. Her trembling hands told him he'd scared and humiliated her.

Same way his old man used to do to him and his siblings. And he got the idea Miss Distraction was like his sister in the way of tears. Rarely did Victoria Reardon cry.

Vic. How he missed her.

Double remorse slugged his gut.

Once for his sister, Victoria.

Once for Valentina Russo.

A protectiveness normally reserved for his sister rose up in Vince for Miss Distraction. He started after her.

Petrowski's strong arm swung out, blocking him. "No. She's upset. Let me go."

Knowing Aaron operated more diplomatically, and not wanting to scare Miss Distraction further, Vince planted his eager feet to the floor and nodded.

On Aaron's way to the door, he paused to peer at Vince. "You didn't hear Stallings explain her reason for the accident, did you?"

"No." In fact, he hadn't wanted to hear. So he'd poked his iPod nubs in his ears and jammed up the volume on his rip-your-ears-off hard rock.

But the terse look in Petrowski's eyes told him he needed to know.

Vince shifted. "What?"

"Her aunt toppled down stairs on a medical scooter. Miss Russo received word of the accident seconds before entering that intersection."

Compassion trickled past the hard earth of Vince's anger. "She all right? The old lady, I mean?"

"Not sure yet. Stallings said she's in surgery again today. So the young woman's understandably under intense pressure right now. Last I heard the aunt was swinging between grave and critical condition."

Petrowski didn't need to say the rest. That Vince needed to go easy on her.

Sorrow settled in. "Aaron, I didn't know, didn't try to. I'll make it right."

Halfway out the door, Petrowski nodded. "I know you will. Mad as you are, your true colors can always be counted on to come through."

That statement stunned Vince. Mostly because he didn't see himself that way and didn't feel he deserved the grace and understanding riding Petrowski's words as he headed to the lot.

In fact, he'd been a complete jerk to Miss Distraction. And for the first time since the wreck, he felt a wiggle of wrong about it.

Vince moved to watch Petrowski leaving out the massive wall of windows that offered a breathtaking panoramic view of the sky he loved to languish in.

An inviting brilliant blue today, it canopied the vast acreage of Refuge Drop Zone's grounds. It housed miles of public and private areas in which they did things as a team for hours each day. Things ranging from rigorous exercise to practicing nighttime military HALO jumps and daytime training to all-out fun with leisure landings.

Adjacent to that closed-off area resided the acreage where they conducted classes meant to train novice skydiving patrons proper body mechanics before they learned to solo or tandem skydive.

The space between Miss Distraction and Petrowski closed rapidly as Aaron sprinted to catch the woman, still rushing across the large lot to her car. She was liable to break her ankle wearing those spiked heels in the gravel part beyond the enormous asphalt section.

It had cost Joel a huge chunk of his savings putting that asphalt in when he'd bought the place after their team stationed in Refuge. Now the team was raising and saving money to help Joel pave the rest.

Why had Miss Distraction parked so far from the building? For exercise maybe? He could tell she did that regularly, too, because a woman didn't get those shapely legs and toned arms solely by being a desk jockey. Not that he'd noticed. Really.

Miss Distraction indeed.

His nickname for her held sudden duplicity. Sure his sarcastic mind had made it up initially because her distraction was the cause of his disaster. But, watching her move in ways he couldn't help but appreciate as a man…*Miss Distraction* took on a whole new meaning.

Vince grew aware of the increasing weight of his teammates' gazes. Choosing to ignore them rather than contend verbally or mentally with what their curious and knowing expressions insinuated, he went to the back room and grabbed his helmet and the keys to his old bike.

"Where you going, dude?" Chance stepped inside the doorway.

"To check on the lady's aunt. I feel bad now for what I said."

"Rain's in the forecast. I'd feel better if you didn't ride your old bike. Le'me drive you."

"Sure you don't mind?"

"Nah. Be glad to. Haven't had lunch, anyway. We'll grab some grub after we go see about the young lady."

"Correction. Her aunt."

Chance jangled his car keys and grinned. "Right."

Vince cradled his helmet in the crook of his elbow and hawkeyed Chance. "Don't make more out of this than it is, Garrison."

Chance's dimples deepened but he pressed the palms of his hands gently in the air. "'Course not."

"I mean it."

Chance laughed as they stepped into the sunshine. He eyed Vince and coughed out a couple more laughs.

Irritation dogged Vince. "Mind telling me what's so funny?"

"She's got your mind all twisted up."

"Does not."

Chance paused, snorting. He dipped his head toward Vince's arm. "Then why do you still have the helmet? My driving's not *that* bad."

Vince pressed his lips together to form a worthy excuse or a solvent retort, but nothing came to mind.

Instead, he felt his own sudden grin give way to an out-loud laugh. His earlobes heated.

Chance stopped. "Wow. Dude. This is a first."

Vince scowled. "What?"

Chance leaned in with focus. "I think you're actually blushing. Wow. The abominable Vince has feelings."

"So what? Everyone gets embarrassed sometimes."

"Really? You've been embarrassed?"

He laughed. "Once."

"When?"

When was the last time he'd been embarrassed? "Eighth grade when snooty girls in class teased me for wearing the same sets of outdated clothes every week, that's when."

"Ah, dude. Kids can be so mean."

"Yeah, well, when there was not enough money for food, new clothes weren't even on the radar." Not on Vince's lawn-mowing and paper-route salaries.

One of the snooty schoolgirls' dads owned a law firm in town, too. Figured.

Sympathy showed in Chance's normally serene eyes. "Sorry, man. I had a good upbringing and loving parents. I can't imagine how hard your childhood was."

The pity in his friend and fellow teammate's voice caused Vince's stomach to ball up into a cringe. "Look, whatever. I'm just…distracted these days." Vince set his helmet on the floorboard of Chance's red Cherokee.

Same shade as Miss Distraction's glimmery lipstick today.

Not that he'd noticed.

Chance tossed his head back and laughed. Good to hear it. Honestly, the guy was so quiet normally it took a vocal excavator to get anything out of his mouth.

The youngest PJ on the team at twenty-five, Chance was painfully shy, but for some reason, not so much around Vince. The two of them plus Brockton, who was a year younger than Vince's twenty-seven, were the only three remaining single guys on the team, so they tended to band together and hang out more these days.

"You know you really shouldn't have thrown that cute little bear."

"Cute?" Vince pulled a face. "You know I'm not into cutesy things."

"Not even the woman?" Chance navigated the Jeep from the DZ lot.

"Not even." Besides, not that he'd admit it to Garrison yet, but the woman was beyond the realm of cute. Make-a-man-gawk gorgeous was more like it. Intelligent eyes. Soothing voice. Authoritative demeanor.

Transparent faith, something he secretly respected in anyone, even if he didn't share it. Bold, heartfelt prayers. She'd talked to God like Joel and Aaron and the rest of the Christians on his team did right before missions. Like God was their friend or something.

Yeah. Miss Distraction was all that. And probably more.

And suddenly, Vince wanted to know the "more."

But, remembering the hurt and humiliation in her vulnerable eyes back at the DZ, he'd likely bombed the foundation of any amicable bridge with her.

And if she were anything like his sister, she'd never cross it on her own. He'd have to make the first move.

Never ever had he such a strong desire to risk those shaky first steps.

"Never ever," Val seethed on the way to her car. Never again would she subject herself to this. She blinked back angry tears.

She'd only seen the man down. The lethal creature storming from the back room looked nothing like the vulnerable one on the road that day in the rain. He'd been intimidating enough that she'd taken two steps back for every step he'd taken toward her.

The man who'd said he was Sarah's fiancé had shaken his head at Vince. Subtle, yet Vince stopped in his tracks. But the look in his eyes said he was none too happy about her being there.

Never would she look back.

Trust Me.

"How? When he can't even stand to look at me?" She flung her rental-car door open and threw herself in the seat. Her hand twisted the key when a knock caused her heart to jump. She removed her hand from her throat and rolled down the window.

Sarah's husband-to-be leaned in. "Miss, I apologize on behalf of Vince."

"He has every right to be angry. I shouldn't have come."

He knelt. "Maybe. Maybe not."

Why did the compassion in his voice cause hers to clog? "Give Sarah my regards. And tell her thank you."

Aaron eyed the DZ then Val. "You could tell her yourself."

Val eyed her clock. Two minutes more and she had to leave. She shut off the ignition. "What are you proposing?"

"Sarah's also new to town. She could use a friend."

"How do you know I'm new?"

"West Coast accent for one thing. For another, your license plates are out of state. Saw your car when I took Vince to check on his bike."

She nodded. "How'd he swallow seeing it?"

Aaron grinned. "How do you think?"

"Probably like a big bowl of razor blades."

He laughed and handed her a business card with caricatures on it. "Give Sarah a call. And give Vince time. His bark is worse than his bite. Most days, anyway."

She laughed. "And that's supposed to make me feel better?"

He smiled. "There are barbecues every weekend at my place or Joel's. Sarah'd love to bring a friend. All the other guys' wives and girlfriends have a good friend. Though they include her, Sarah is shy and feels like a fifth wheel. That she spoke to you at all proves she felt a connection with you."

"Interesting. I felt that with her, too."

"I'll let her know you'll be calling."

She shielded her eyes from the southern Illinois sun and met his gaze. "Why do I get the feeling you want me to try to get through to Vince?"

A confident gleam entered his eyes. "Probably for the same reason that I get the feeling you *can.*"

His words paused her heart and soul.

Get through to him she wanted to. But only God could move the mountain of this man's anger toward her and all that she stood for. Vince's face flashed in her mind.

No matter how hard, she would obey.

"I'll give Sarah a call."

"And I'll give her a heads-up that you'll be coming to the barbecue."

"Hey, now. All I said was that I'd call."

"Prayerfully consider it. It'll mean a lot to her to have another woman to pal around with."

"How do you know I pray?"

He snorted. "Trust me, Vince let us know."

"Speaking of Vince, will you be warning him that I'm coming? You know, in case he wants to stay home or fling himself in front of a moving planet or otherwise orbit himself out of his misery."

Aaron chuckled. "What he doesn't know won't hurt him." He knuckled her door frame. "Besides, he drowns his misery in Michelob."

"Ah. The old alcohol vice."

"Yeah, he pretty much never leaves home without it. He always drinks at the barbecues, which means he's normally more subdued, which could be good for you. And as long as he doesn't try to drive himself home, we don't give him too much grief. We know God'll change him when Vince finally gives himself over to Him."

"If I show up without warning he'll know he's been set up."

"So be it. But you have no less than seven third-degree black-belted bodyguards, guaranteed."

She laughed. "That should make me feel better."

His grin faded and his face turned serious. "He might scare the daylights out of you. But he'd never in a million years hurt you. At least not physically."

What did that mean? Vince was a heartbreaker?

"Well, I have no intention of getting close to him that way." He'd never let her, for one thing. For another, he far from acted like a Christian.

Petrowski studied her so carefully that the urge to win the case of convincing him overpowered her.

"Trust me. You don't have to worry about me falling for the guy or him falling for me. He strikes me as the type who goes from zero to mad in three-point-five seconds. And I'm so laid-back I'm horizontal."

She shook her head and started her car. "The Mississippi would move backward before the two of us would fall for one another."

Petrowski laughed. "It's happened before, you know."

"What? A woman like me falling for a man like Vince? Or a man like Vince falling for a woman like me?"

"I meant the Mississippi running backward."

"Really, now?"

"Yup. During an earthquake along the New Madrid fault."

Even so, it was going to take something stronger than her to run the river of this man's rage away from her rather than toward. After arriving home, Val set down her briefcase, called to check on Elsie, left Sarah a voice mail then climbed into bed.

Creator of heaven and earth, move the mountain of this man's anger.

The next day at the hospital, violent shaking rattled Val's water glass off the table beside Elsie's bed. She shot up, eyeing Val with fear from her transfer chair.

"It's okay, Elsie." At least Val hoped so. The floor swayed several inches left and right and left and right. She pushed Elsie toward the doorway barely comprehending what this was.

Earthquakes in southern Illinois? She'd experienced—even expected them—in California. Never in her wildest dreams would she have thought they'd have them here.

The early-morning shimmy concluded by the time she crouched in the doorway beside Elsie's chair and knelt with her Bible to her chest. She hadn't even realized she'd grabbed it. The pendulum-swinging floor paused. Elsie drew a relieved breath and relaxed her grip from the chair.

Val exited Elsie's room to find people in the hall looking bedraggled and confused. "Earthquake?" Val asked.

A family member to Elsie's hospital neighbor to the left approached. "Yeah. Worst one I recall in years."

"So this isn't normal?"

"Not really. Quakes that size are extremely rare."

Val recalled her conversation with Aaron.

And burst out laughing.

A single mom Val recognized from her neighborhood and who had a teen named Logan approached. "You probably think we're amateurs because you're from California, huh?"

Val wondered what the woman was doing at the hospital. "No, that's not it. I just found it ironic that I had a conversation mere hours ago about earthquakes."

Earthquakes...a woman like her falling for a man like Vince.

Never happen. Not in a million years.

Petrowski's and her words wafted back into her mind. Val eyed the sky through the window back inside Elsie's room. *I hope this isn't a foreshadowing of things to come. But I'll consider myself sufficiently warned.* Elsie eyed her curiously but didn't ask.

* * *

After waking before her alarm clock in the morning, Val flung the covers off and prepared to go visit Aunt Elsie again.

Her phone rang. A number she didn't recognize popped up. "Hello," she answered, not giving her name. Since she was a prosecutor, she kept her name, numbers and addresses unlisted.

"Yes, I'm Sarah Graham and I'm returning Val Russo's call."

"Sarah! Hey, this is Val."

"I wanted to catch you before you rushed off to work. I hope it's not too early."

"No, today is Wednesday so I work through client files from home." Val caught sight of her hair in the mirror on the way to get her clothes. "Ew! What a fright."

"The files?"

Val laughed. "No, I know better than to go to bed with wet hair. But frankly, yesterday left me mentally and physically exhausted."

"Aaron told me."

Val developed an instant liking to Sarah and was determined to build a friendship. She got ready as they chattered on and on.

"Hopefully today will be a better day for Elsie," Val said into her cell to Sarah on her way out the door.

"And for you," Sarah said with a chuckle.

Val adjusted her rearview mirror. "As long as I

don't have another run-in with a certain tall, dark and dangerous special operative who's homicidally livid over losing his bike, I think I'll be okay."

Sarah laughed. "I better let you go since you're heading to the hospital. And we know what happened the last time you drove while talking on a phone."

Val sighed. "Yes, but thankfully I have a hands-free now. Still, I better sign off. Promise to call you later."

"Especially since I have a feeling you will see Tall, Dark and Dangerous again." Sarah made an exaggerated throat-clearing noise.

"Is that a drastic hint that you know something I don't?" Val pulled out of her driveway.

"Yes, but this time, you don't need to be afraid. You'll want to hear what he's coming to say."

Chapter Five

Val felt Vince's approach before she saw him.

Her heart began to pound, but not just from fear. More from the fact that he'd actually made an effort to come talk to her for the third day in a row.

She'd missed his visit yesterday, but when she'd called Sarah-soon-to-be-Petrowski, she'd casually mentioned that Vince had tried to find Val after she'd left the DZ that first day, then again at the hospital yesterday.

That he'd been actively trying to find her caused her heart to speed in ways that ought to be illegal.

His massive presence consumed the hallway and her senses as he moved silently to stand next to where she stood in front of an ICU window. "Why didn't you tell me?" he said without looking at her.

"What?" Val stared straight ahead, too. His nearness exuded barely chained power. But she didn't get the idea his persona housed hostility as much as it did passion for whatever he'd come here to say to her.

He stood probably three, four inches away, but the warmth coming from his arm next to hers gave the comfortable illusion that their arms were touching.

The strangest sensation went through her that some kind of unexpected bond had formed between them that day in the intersection. She'd glued her gaze to his eyes and refused to look away or stop praying despite his carefully compressed anger and his spoken and unspoken protest.

She felt it now, the invisible draw linking them. Only this time his resistance wasn't paramount. He was surprisingly calm.

Hopefully not the kind of calm that a hurricane conceals in its eye right before the back wall blasts whatever's in its path.

"If your aunt was hurt and asking for you, you should have been there."

"I had a hard choice. I don't know if I made the right one. But I know my aunt knows the Lord and He would have been with her in my place. You, I wasn't sure about. I caused the accident, so it was only right for me to stay and make sure you were okay."

"You sat there silent and let me lambaste you for talking on the phone. You coulda told me you had a family emergency." He stuffed his hands in his front jeans pockets. His wide shoulders raised and lowered in a sigh.

Frustration?

Since he was being honestly vulnerable, she'd be vulnerably honest.

She knew without a doubt that he was the kind of guy who could more than effectively hide anything he was feeling or thinking. That he didn't choose to do that around her caused a blip of hope to flash across the radar of her intent to befriend him.

"I was concerned about you." She repositioned from facing the glass to facing him.

His left eye flinched. His face hardened. He shifted as if to turn away from her caring gaze. In fact, he stared at her face the way Dracula might stare at a raised wooden stake. Interesting.

She tilted her head. "Is that some big sin, Vince?"

His eyes narrowed. "What?"

"Why do you have such trouble letting someone care about you?"

His jaw clenched and his expression changed so that he now looked at her as though convinced she were a certified loon. "You know nothing about me. And you made a bad call that day, lady." He hiked a chin toward the partition of curtains which they both knew housed her aunt. "She needed you. You shoulda been there for her."

"I chose you, Vince. Not out of guilt, not out of obligation. But because I cared what happened to you."

"You don't know me. Because if you did, you'd care only to run hard and fast the other way." He turned to go. Looked like he could run, in fact.

Go was the last thing she wanted Vince to do. She

rushed forward. Put her hand on his arm. "Vince, wait."

Her hand on his arm stopped him. Though his back was to her, he angled so she saw his darkening chiseled profile.

"Why don't you let me get to know you and then we'll see." The words rushed out of her in a jumble.

He half snorted, half laughed, but turned to stare at her. "You're a real piece of work. You know that?"

"Let me in, Vince." No clue what compelled her to say it.

He tilted his head in a peculiar not-sure-I-heard-you-right manner. "What?"

She stepped closer. "Let me get to know you. And we'll see if I want to run hard and fast."

He said nothing for a full minute. Just stared at her as though she'd lost her mind. And quite frankly, she wondered the same.

Then a trouble-making grin spread across his face. But latent curiosity embedded deeper ruined the sordid effect she could tell he was going for. "You're no shrinking violet. That's for sure." Looks of sedated wonder and humored interest piqued on his normally stony face.

She struck a lawyer pose. "I'm being serious here."

He gave a short laugh. "Sounds like a challenge."

"Maybe it is. And you don't strike me as the kind of guy who backs off from anything, especially not a challenge."

"Don't play with me, lady. Bottom line."

"Fine. This isn't about a challenge. This is about us getting to know one another."

His mouth curled into a smile that suggested more.

"As *friends*," she quickly added.

"No ulterior motive?"

"None."

He shifted his stance and eyed her from a different angle. "You're not trying to recruit me to your faith?"

She shrugged. "No."

Suspicion clouded his eyes. "Because my teammates, they're falling like dominoes into the Christian faith and always trying to convert me. It's weirding me out. And you strike me as their type."

"No agenda. I want to be your friend. Period."

His head twitched back. "I don't need friends."

"You don't *want* to need them, but you do. Besides, you have friends. They stayed at the hospital worried sick about you when they heard about your accident."

He scowled but listened.

"So there must be something about you to love, Vince, because I saw a throng of people in that waiting room and pacing the halls who love you."

"Wait. You came to the hospital to see me?"

"Yes. Although I didn't have guts to approach you."

That made him laugh. But his smile quickly faded as he shook his head. "Those people you saw, that's my pararescue team. They tolerate me because they have no choice. We're assigned together."

"Liar. They have a choice. It goes beyond your role on the PJ team. They love you, even though you're brooding, stubborn and obstinate."

"Stubborn and obstinate? Well now. Looks like we have something in common." Speaking of looks, his stormy eyes did a commando crawl across her face and down to her lips.

Suddenly he looked like all he wanted to do was kiss her. "Fine," he said. "It's on."

"Yes," she whispered sarcastically. "The battle of the century."

Especially if he ever looked at her like that again.

"Indeed," Vince agreed and eyed the window. "You need to go in there and be with your aunt?"

Val shook her head. "I spent the morning with her. She needs to rest now."

"She gonna be all right?"

"She's improving. Doctors are hopeful." Val faced him and again he was struck by her beauty. Normally he preferred tattooed, pierced, Harley-riding party girls who dressed in formfitting denim and slick leather. Not the kind of woman, like Val, who looked polished, poised and put together. All business every second of the day, like she didn't have a wild hair on her head.

But actually, her hair was spiky and trendy and her clothes modern-edgy. Though conservative, she was out-on-the-edge stylish. And for once, that appealed to him.

Down at the end of the hall, Chance came off the elevator and leaned against the wall waiting for Vince. He watched the two of them carefully, but not so openly as to be rude. Just like a casual observer.

Val peered at Chance over her shoulder. "We're under surveillance."

Her humor caught Vince off guard. He laughed. Nodded. "I see that."

"I remember seeing him at the skydiving facility. What's his name?"

"Chance. Don't be offended if he doesn't say two words. He's shy. And the term for a skydiving facility is a Drop Zone or just DZ." Vince waved Chance over.

"Ah. You seem proficient in street lingo. Maybe you could teach me some."

Vince snorted as Chance meandered down the hall. "And why would a do-gooder like you want to know street lingo?"

She shrugged and twirled her hair. "Have my reasons."

Chance, now paused and talking on a cell phone, held up a finger, which meant he'd be there in a second.

Vince laughed.

"What's funny?" Val smiled to match his laughter. Probably because she knew it was so uncharacteristic of him.

"I guarantee he's giving Joel and Petrowski intel on us. And they're probably ordering Chance to stick close enough to step in and referee if need be."

She giggled. And the throaty sound made its way inside him. Caused his pulse to rev like his bike on full throttle down a stretch of empty southern Illinois road.

She eyed Chance but faced Vince. "They know you're here?"

"They know I came to see you yesterday, but you were tied up with your aunt. So I figured you'd be back today."

"How did you know what time?"

"Lucky guess."

"Lucky guess?"

"I figure you for a creature of habit. Figured you'd come the same time every day. Am I right?"

Her mouth dropped open. But she straightened and closed it. Her arms crossed over her chest and a look of consternation came over her face.

"Thought so." He started to walk toward Chance, who now approached.

Val reached out her hand. "Hi, Chance. I'm Valentina Russo. Friends call me Val. I remember you from the DZ."

Wordlessly, Chance enveloped her hand and nodded.

"Did you brief the guys that Val's still in one piece?" Vince smirked.

Mildly blushing, Chance eyed Val and grinned. "Something like that."

"Ready to grab some grub?" Vince slung his arm over Chance's shoulder. "Pal?"

"Yeah. Coming with?" Chance asked Val.

Vince dropped his arm and stare-glared at Chance, who never said more than six words at a time, period. Not even to his friends. Yet here he was inviting the Enemy to what was supposed to be an exclusively male lunch.

No worries. Not like she'd ever accept the invitation to be near a brooding grump anyway. Not for more time than necessary beyond whatever philanthropist ideals she had giving her crazy notions about attempting friendship. It wouldn't last long.

Val looked to be chewing on Chance's invitation. Maybe he'd help her out. "I'm sure she has better things to do today. She's a busy woman with an important job. All those real criminals out there that she has to figure out how to let off when innocent people don't go free."

Her gasp siphoned all the air from the lobby as they walked toward the hospital exit. Her lips pressed together and her eyes grew even smokier.

Uh-oh. Maybe he'd ticked her off. He grinned.

Finally, she raised her chin. "Actually, I think I would love to join you for lunch. I'm rather hungry."

No way. No way did she just accept the lunch invitation. Especially not after the verbal slam he'd not-so-subtly sent her way.

Chance eyed one then the other and burst out laughing. He clamped a hand on Vince's shoulder. "I do believe, *pal,* that you have met your match."

Vince clenched his teeth. What was the worst dive of a roach-infested restaurant that he could take her to that would surely drive her off?

Vince shot Chance a dirty look that would leave no doubt that he was not happy about him inviting Miss Distraction to their dinner.

Chance not only ignored Vince, but he had the audacity to grin as he opened the door for Val once they got to the Cherokee. Vince swept aside the swim-safety manuals and gear so he could sit in the back and let Val ride shotgun in the front. With Chance.

The swim items reminded him that he needed to do some last-minute planning with Chance to be sure they were set with safety equipment needed to start the community swim program that Refuge City Hall asked them to do on Monday.

"Where are we eating?" Val asked as they pulled from the lot.

"Biker bar on the square. Although you're over-dressed," Vince said before Chance could speak.

"You mean Talons?" Chance eyed Vince in the rearview mirror.

Vince grinned sadistically. "Yeah."

Now Chance reciprocated Vince's dirty look. "Nah, now that's no place to bring a lady."

Pivoting in her seat, Val issued Vince a challenging gleam. "Actually, if Vince would like to eat there, I'm up for it."

Vince smirked and held her sparring gaze.

She knew.

Knew he'd picked it just to tick her off.

Only it wasn't working. His smirk faded with defeat.

Well, when she saw that Talons, the raunchy biker bar, was not only a smoke dive that housed loud offensive music, nasty ashtrays, the biggest stash of hard liquor in Refuge and the most debaucherous crowd in town, she'd likely never speak to him again.

Vince's grin returned. This just might work to get her off his back. "Fine. Talons it is."

Val felt like twitching when she left the bar and grill—which had mostly been a bar. She blinked eyes, scratchy from smoke that was its own entity in the pub.

The scantily-clad woman who'd been their waitress had nearly done her in, though. Especially the seven-inch spiked heels the woman apparently thought were "work-appropriate attire." No tofu or pomegranate green tea in sight. And when Val'd asked to see a vegetarian menu, the waitress had snorted and walked off laughing.

No matter. She'd survived. And obviously to the surprise of Vince, who actually hadn't finished even the first glass of beer. And the owner, who seemed well-acquainted with Vince, had brought out an entire pitcher of the amber froth-topped stuff.

She checked her watch as they approached Chance's car. "Next time, you pick the food place," Val said to him.

He grinned. "Told you. Talons is no place for a lady." He lowered his voice and raised his gaze to Vince, who chatted with one of the waitresses on the other side of the car. "Although I think you surprised him. Most women of your caliber would have fled after five minutes."

The woman handed Vince a piece of paper, saying, "Bye, handsome."

Val averted her gaze.

"He'll never call her." Chance held the door open while Val climbed in.

She paused to stare at him. Why had Chance felt it important to tell her that? More concerning, why did it make her feel better to know Vince might just be showing interest in the waitress to rile or repel Val?

She eyed her watch. She had to get some more work done today for an upcoming trial. She hadn't expected this little lunch detour. But her car was still at the hospital, on the other side of town. "Would you mind dropping me by my office on the way to my car?"

"No problem." Chance navigated them down the streets of Refuge.

"The address is 1212 Justice Street."

Vince snorted. "Justice. Why does that not surprise me?" His face darkened and his mood turned tart.

Chance pulled into the parking lot of the county prosecutor's office. She jogged inside.

Val's young secretary, training to be a jury profiler,

handed Val her messages. "You have a witness interview scheduled next Tuesday. And a lady named Sarah called to see how it went."

"Oh, good. She's a new friend I met."

Her secretary peered over fashionable glasses. "I admit I'm wondering what 'it' is."

Laughing, Val placed the messages in her blue briefcase. "You're insatiably curious. I had lunch with Vince Reardon."

"Oh, that brooding air force guy? The cute one."

"Yes, but he's a party animal and a player. So for the record, I'm not interested romantically. The only thing I'm interested in is to develop a program to keep teenagers out of trouble."

"Yeah, so how's the teen thing going?"

"The wreck threw a wrench into my plans to open a youth center. But I came up with several activities to take them to. In fact, one starts Monday at Refuge Community Pool. Free water-safety and swim lessons."

The phone rang. "Well, good luck with that."

Val stepped out as her secretary took the call.

Vince didn't look at or verbally acknowledge her as she reentered the car. Nor did he say a word on the way to the hospital. Chance made small talk. And while Vince would acknowledge Chance, he completely ignored Val.

And it bothered her more than she cared to know why. Reminded her of times her dad was constantly on business calls. Never able to leave work at work and make home a home. The only time he'd paid her any mind was when she'd started voicing interest in entering his law field.

He hadn't even broken away from work to come see his own sister when she'd tumbled down the steps on her scooter. It hadn't seemed to bother Elsie as much as it had Val, though. Elsie said she knew he was married to his work.

Val stared at the work in her lap.

And here she was doing the same thing.

Not only an attorney, but bringing her work home.

Oh, well. Not like she had a family at home who'd feel neglected. Once she had the family she longed for, she'd leave work firmly at work.

"Thanks for lunch." Val grabbed her papers as Chance pulled up next to her car. Vince still hadn't said two words to her the entire trip home. The methodical ignoring was probably another tactic to make himself look rude.

"Sure." Chance started to get out, probably to open her door.

She waved him back. "I got it." She faced Vince, who now studied her carefully.

"I had a rather...interesting...time. Thanks for paying for my lunch."

Vince smirked. "I didn't. Chance picked up your tab."

Her cheeks heated. After all, why on earth would she assume for one second Vince would pay for her meal? It wasn't like they'd gone on a date or something.

She clutched her papers closer and exited the car truly flustered. Maybe he wouldn't notice.

With Vince, maybe she'd bitten off more than she could chew. He seemed so hardened. Maybe she was foolhardy to think she could crack him. Maybe she should just stick to reaching out to teens.

She cast a glance over her shoulder, hoping to catch a glimpse of Vince watching her, waving, nodding goodbye. Something. But no.

Nothing.

He didn't meet her gaze. Never even looked her way as Chance, waving, backed out.

She waved to Chance then eyed Vince through the windshield.

Like the glass, he seemed coated in shatterproof material. As hard as she could kick, she might never break through to him.

If there's hope, give it to me. Because right now, things look pretty bleak.

Val had no idea how she'd even contact him again. What would she even say to him? "Let's do lunch at Talons again?"

She called Sarah and gave her the lowdown. Sarah issued a compassionate sigh. "Don't let the way Vince acted discourage you, Val. If this is God, there'll be another common ground. He'll crack in and make a way."

Chapter Six

"No way." Vince gritted his teeth and tossed a life jacket at the concrete wall of Refuge's indoor swimming pool the next Monday. "You've got to be kidding me."

Chance looked up in time to join Vince in seeing Val get out of a van which spilled a dozen teenagers.

Chance laughed. "I think she's stalking you, dude."

"Not hardly. She's not the stalking type. Trust me."

"Think she knows you're here?"

Vince snorted. "Doubt it. The way I treated her during the Talons lunch, I wouldn't blame her if she never spoke to me again."

Chance cocked his head. "So, just out of curiosity, did you ever call the waitress?"

What was he talking about? Vince blinked at Chance then stared back out the window at Val, who ushered the truant-looking teens and their towels from the van.

"What waitress?" Vince asked.

"Yeah. That's what I thought."

What was Chance yammering about? For that matter, *why* was he? Dude never talked. Never.

"So, next question. Did you think about Miss Distraction this weekend?" Chance strung a lifeguard whistle around his neck and handed Vince one.

"You picked a fine time to loose those introverted lips, Garrison. Let's get ready for swim class. By the way, you take Miss Distraction's crowd."

"I already told the seniors' club I'd be in charge of their water aerobics and arthritis-pain-management swim class today."

Vince knelt and felt the water temperature. "Come on. Do me this one favor. Don't make me take Miss Distraction and her mighty minions into my class."

"You do well with teens. You scare old people. With all those black back tattoos, the kids will think you're cool." Chance grinned. "Besides, I enjoy watching you interact with Miss Distraction."

"Remind me never to share my secrets with you again, Garrison." Vince stood back from the side of the pool and pulled off his T-shirt. Why he'd shared his nickname for Val with Chance, he didn't know. But these days he and Chance and Brock were all buddy-buddy. So it seemed like the thing to do.

But now, his opening up was coming back to bite him.

Val looked up just then as she stepped through the door and came toward the pool. The look of total shock on her face at seeing him quickly turned to horror as she tripped over a duffel bag and fell forward...

"Oh, no!" Chance's arms jerked up, which struck Vince funny since they were too far away to catch her. "She's going in—"

Splash!

Vince rushed forward, dove in to the deep end and swam to her. She'd fallen into the shallow end. Business suit and all.

She floundered face-first near the bottom. A person could stand up and the water was no deeper than waist-high on an adult. Had she hit her head or neck?

That could paralyze a person. Why wasn't she coming up? Vince lunged to the bottom, grabbed her by the soggy shoulders and jerked her up while trying to protect her head and neck.

She came up sputtering.

And mad.

Hands to her shoulders, Vince let out a deep breath. "You okay?"

She blinked and coughed. Her face reddened. From embarrassment or anger, he wasn't sure.

He looked her over. No visible injuries.

"Let go of me." She jerked from his grasp and tried to wobble toward the edge of the pool. He dropped his chin and eyed his hands, which were trembling.

What on earth? He never got nervous.

He also noticed that Miss Distraction held one

dripping heel in her hand. Probably she'd been facedown looking for the other, since she limped.

Leave it to a woman to care more about her endangered high-end shoe than any potential water filling her lungs.

She'd be the death of him yet.

He reached down in the water, found and rescued her other shoe. Then followed her up the pool steps.

An undignified grating sound came from her throat and her arms flew up in the air as she faced the teens. "Go ahead and laugh. I know you all want to." She flung wet hair off her forehead.

One by one they started giggling.

On approach, Vince rested a hand on her shoulder. "Here's your shoe."

Her face softened. "Thanks."

"Nice dive by the way." He sucked his cheek in to keep from laughing.

She planted her free hand on her soaked hip and narrowed her eyes at him. "Smart aleck." She hooked her finger through the strappy sandal he held and pulled.

He held. Grinned.

She jerked, tried to step away. Her hose snagged on the rough concrete around the pool and a run ripped through the stockings of very nice legs.

The pool manager walked up toting a whistle and a clipboard just then. "Miss Russo?"

Val wrung water from her hair and stepped forward.

"That would be me."

The squat woman eyed her up and down. "Most people put on swimming suits first."

"Ha-ha. I went in by accident."

The manager, a boisterous blonde with bright eyes who, by dress, looked more like a referee than a pool employee, gave a hearty chuckle. "Well, if you are accident prone around water, you came to the right place." She pointed her clipboard at Vince. "And you are in good hands."

Val's head snapped up. "Excuse me?" Her face paled.

Vince pulled his favorite extra towel off a peg on the wall and handed it to Val, hoping she'd remember to give it back.

She stared at it and him in trepidation.

"It's clean and dry. And you're sopping."

"Good point." She took the towel. "So, what does she mean by *I'm in good hands*?" She bit her lip and squished her sculpted eyebrows together.

"I'm one of the community swim instructors."

Her mouth opened and then clamped shut. A disturbed look began to brew in her eyes. "Oh."

"Trust me, I didn't plan this either." He started to walk away.

She rushed forward. "Wait. I didn't mean to be rude. I'm sure you're perfectly capable of giving swim-safety classes. And...I appreciate the towel."

He nodded. Then turned away.

She fell into step beside him. Felt weird. Having her suddenly at his side. Like an ally.

Only she was, because of her Christian and attorney status, still by all intents and purposes, the Enemy.

He walked faster. Tried to lose her.

She sped up, kept up. Athletic woman.

"You'll be glad to know that I'm not the one taking lessons. They are." She waved toward the wall of teens standing around the pool manager who was taking down their names.

Vince eyed her wet attire. "Sure you don't need swim lessons, too?" He issued a razzing smile.

"I hadn't planned on going into the water."

His smile faded. "Yeah. Life has a way of bringing the unwanted."

Unwanted.

Val's heart honed in on that word. Her hostility toward Vince suddenly melted because in that spoken word rested remnants of the pain she'd witnessed. Deep in his eyes the day of the wreck as he lay bleeding in the road. The day God had pulled back a veil and allowed her, for whatever reason, to glimpse a wounded spirit.

Wounded by the loss of his brother. But was there more?

She didn't know. But she had a sense that whatever it was happened both recently and long ago.

Her resolve to help Vince renewed in a wave of mercy that filtered around her, engulfing her spirit just as the water had surrounded her skin when she fell into the pool.

She drew a breath of knowing that no matter how difficult he became, she would not relent in her mercy toward him. Maybe she was meant to be a reflection of God's devotion of mercy toward Vince. Devotion that didn't wane depending on Vince's readiness to receive it.

She stepped toward where he spoke to the kids about pool safety. She eyed the large tribal tattoo on his broad back and realized that it was in the shape of a motorcycle.

Which made her mind up to try even harder to get in touch with his sister. She'd managed to get a name from Joel. But the first few numbers she'd called weren't Vince's sister.

In fact... "You'll keep an eye on the kids?" Val asked Vince. He nodded then joined the pool manager.

Val went to the rented van and obtained her briefcase, then returned to seat herself in one of the poolside chairs. She peeled off her sodden jacket and draped it over the chair arm. She tugged a yellow legal pad from her briefcase onto her lap and poised her pen.

Making sure Vince was out of earshot, she continued down her list. Who knew there were so many Victoria Reardons in the world?

Pushing off her sandals and wiggling her toes, Val flipped over her papers. Clicked her pen. There had to be hundreds of leads. She'd call every single one and use her Westlaw program if she had to in order to reach Vince's sister. It'd help if she knew the state Victoria currently resided in.

She slipped her feet back into her sandals and adjusted her toe ring so the sapphire flower faced upward. She liked everything orderly. And this phone call process was less than.

She eyed Vince. No. She couldn't ask him for the number because then he'd be onto her plan and may sever ties with Val altogether.

Vince led the teens to the safety gear. He looked so patient working with the kids. And the kids seemed engaged in whatever he was saying and showing them.

Val flipped open her phone and started dialing the next number on her list.

By the time the teens stepped out of the shallow end at the end of their first lesson, Val had phoned well over fifty of the numbers.

Disappointment dogged her.

Not one hit. Not at least of the ones she spoke to. The others, she simply left a message for them to call her.

Val placed her things back in her powder-blue briefcase as Vince dismissed the teens, who headed to the locker rooms to change.

Val approached where he knelt, rearranging pool noodles or whatever those foam floaties were called.

"How'd it go?" she asked.

"Fine."

"Did they have fun?"

Vince shrugged and didn't look at her.

"Have you been a swim instructor a long time?"

"Depends."

"On what?"

"Stuff."

Okay. So maybe she should ask some open-ended questions.

He began hanging safety gear in its place on the pool wall. He never spoke to her.

"What made you decide to help people learn swim safety?"

"It's complicated." He knelt and pushed shoes to the side of the wall. He still didn't look at her.

"Did you volunteer?"

He rose and flashed a look of irritation her way. "You sure ask a lot of questions. What is this, a deposition?"

Her face flushed hot with anger.

No. No, she would not let him get to her. "Of course not. I'm interested in the program, is all." *Interested in you, really.* But she dare not say that to him lest he take it the wrong way.

"Well?" She followed him down the length of the pool. He walked fast, as if trying to get away from her. She rushed to keep up and rested his towel over his tanned arm.

"Well, what?" He flung his towel over his shoulder.

"How did you get into volunteerism?"

"Bridge collapse."

"I heard about Refuge's bridge collapse on the news. Seems I recall a pararescue team was first on the scene. Was that you?"

"Yup."

"Do you have kids of your own?"

"Nope."

"What do you do for fun?"

"Jump."

"How long have you been a PJ?"

His eyebrows slashed downward as he scowled over his shoulder. "Look, I got better things to do than undergo the rigors of legal questioning. So, if you're done—"

"Legal quest—?" She threw up her hands. "Never mind. I give up. Obviously you're not paying attention to what I'm saying. Because if you were, you'd realize that I'm just trying to make small talk. To assemble a strand of peace between us since we got off on bad footing. But you're not paying attention to me, period."

Hot tears of frustration burned behind her eyes, mostly because she'd foolishly blurted all that, thinking wrongly that he'd care. She turned to go. Dignity and all.

Flashes of movement behind her and a firm grip on her forearm stopped her.

She tilted her face up to find Vince's inches away.

For a moment they just stood there. He leaned in. So close she knew if the teens came out now, this would look much too intimate. But his intense look locked her there.

"The arch of your left foot is noticeably higher than your right. You have a two-inch surgical scar on your right elbow, probably from a sports accident in high school. You're wearing sparkly toenail polish that matches the pink jewels on the phone you've used exactly sixty-four times since you sat in the fourth lounger on the left."

Her eyes widened.

He stepped closer. "You lean forward and slightly to the left when you smile even though you're right-handed. You have a blue ring on the middle toe of your left foot that matches the watch you spin while you work. You sit with one knee crossed over the other and pump your calves when you're talking on the phone."

Spellbound, she gulped.

He moved another step closer. "And you giggled behind your hand every time one of the kids splashed me in the face."

Utterly flummoxed, she swallowed.

He dropped his gaze to her face and lowered his voice. He stood so near that his cheek nearly grazed hers and his lips rested a whisper from her earlobe. "Now, are you *sure* that I don't pay *close* attention?"

Close.

Gulp. Gulp. Gulp.

He was *so* close.

And she was *so* flustered by his nearness.

Imposing. Magnetic. Dizzying.

Overpowering. Like strong cologne. Only he wore none.

She gulped.

Any moment now, she'd morph into a guppy.

He inclined his head toward the teens' belongings. "You asked if I volunteered for this." He returned his gaze to her. One side of his suddenly-appealing mouth lifted in what might be a smile. Looked for a moment like he might be vulnerable. Might really want to know. "What do *you* think?"

When breath came back to her she lifted her chin and matched his gaze. "I think you did. But I think you don't want to admit it to me." The words came out as a breathy whisper. And she didn't care that she appeared vulnerable as well.

Vince stared into her eyes a moment longer, face unreadable except for a glisten of something. Some unspoken message of approval. Respect? The connection surged between them again.

It might be attraction but seemed more like respect.

She'd earned his and maybe he'd earned hers.

Just then he stepped calmly back and let her hand go.

She hadn't realized until that moment he still held it. She missed the contact. Hadn't expected such a strong, hard man to have such warm, tender hands.

Seconds later the teens, giggling and laughing

rather than the usual sulking and complaining, rushed in a chaotic line from the changing rooms.

How had Vince known they were about to come out? Ultra-acute hearing and senses? And how had he noticed all those details about her and still kept an ultra-watchful eye on each of the teens?

No wonder You wanted him to be a pararescuer. His gifts perfectly align with his creed and his career.

Respect ramped as Val watched Vince approach the changing room.

He is astonishingly gifted, Lord. Help him to realize that. And to fulfill completely the destiny You have for him.

Peace befell her. As did an acute sense of someone watching her. Where had Chance gone? Val tugged her collar around her neck and surveyed the pool.

Chance knelt in the corner watching her then Vince, who also eyed her over his shoulder. The two men exchanged glances with one another. An amused look dominated Chance's face and brightened his trademark shy, lopsided grin. Vince shook his head at Chance and hardened his jaw.

Trying to shake off a slightly flustered feeling at being the object of an unspoken conversation, Val gathered the teens around her. "Okay, find your stuff. Then we'll plan who wants to be picked up for the next outing."

They scrambled for shoes, backpacks and duffel bags then approached.

Val tugged her notebook from her briefcase. Pen

poised, she asked, "So, who wants to come for another swimming lesson next week?"

All hands went up.

She laughed. Because when she'd put fliers up and handed them out in her neighborhood, most of the teens had scoffed at the idea of going swimming.

But a dozen of them had shown up.

"So you all are returning. Can you think of others who might want to join us next week?"

"Yeah!" Several teens threw out names.

Val handed them legal forms. "I've got medical forms and permission slips on each of you. But I'll need them signed by a guardian of anyone you invite.

"I can take up to eighteen on that van I'm renting. Which means six of you can invite someone."

"How much will it cost?" one teen asked.

"Not a dime." Val wrote each of their names down, but there were more names than slots. A good problem to have.

Freshly showered and in street clothes, Vince approached just then.

"What if we all want to invite someone?" a teen named Logan asked.

Val blinked. "Then I guess I'd have to get help and rent a bigger van."

Vince studied her carefully. Then stepped away.

"We still doing the pizza thing?" Julio, the tall, lanky teen asked as Vince returned with Chance.

"Sure are." Suddenly remembering the legal pad had Vince's sister's name on every line for ten pages, and how acutely perceptive Vince was of details, Val slipped the notepad back in her briefcase. More like, shoved it.

If he'd seen his sister's name on the pad, he didn't let on. Even so, her heart pounded all the way to the van as she herded the teens toward it.

Chance helped elderly swimmers to their vehicles. Vince waved goodbye to the kids.

But not to her.

Which meant he still hadn't completely forgiven her for the wreck.

Would he ever?

Chapter Seven

Val brought her neighborhood brood back to the pool as she had for the past three weeks. The sight of Vince enthusiastically greeting the kids stirred something inside her. Longing?

If so, for what?

To have that kind of a reception? To know him better? Seeing this softer side of him surprised her. He seemed less hostile and far from aloof today. Even nodded a greeting her way when she brought the teens in. An abrupt nod, but still a nod. Progress, right?

Which, she hoped meant he'd softened more toward her, too.

Logan approached Val after the swim lesson. "Can we ask the swim teacher to go?" Logan's speech seemed particularly despondent and he hadn't swum today.

"You mean Vince?" she asked Logan.

He nodded and raised his arm to scoop stringy hair from his eyes. The motion revealed a brownish-yellow splotch surrounded by round red pockmarks. It shone beneath the cuff of his jacket.

Concern streaked through her.

She reached for his wrist. Logan angled his arm away and tugged his sleeves down. A struggle since the jacket looked three sizes too small.

What kid wore a jacket indoors?

One trying to hide injuries?

A sick feeling roiled in her gut.

Had Vince noticed, too? Should she mention it? Val eyed Vince, who was leaving the change room with Chance. Moments later Vince walked past without acknowledging her, then talked to a cluster of nearby kids.

"Um, I honestly doubt he'd go, Logan." She didn't want Logan to be disappointed. She had a feeling his life was rough enough already.

Logan blinked at Vince then her. "Why?"

Julio approached. "Yeah, why?"

"I—er…" *He wants little to do with me.* "He's a very busy man."

Vince looked over his shoulder. Studied her and Logan. *Very* carefully. Was he within hearing range?

"Yeah, like my old man. Always too busy for me." Julio scowled. Logan's shoulders drooped.

Vince's face softened more than she'd ever dreamed it could. He said something to Chance, who followed him the few feet over to Val.

"Dude, she says you're too busy to hang with us," Julio said in accusatory tones.

"Did she now?" Vince slid a crooked grin at her.

Val's cheeks heated. "I said you were a very busy person. You have important things to do."

Vince eyed her then the teens. "Nothing more important than hanging with you guys." His gaze honed in especially on Logan. And Julio. The teen boys tended to gravitate toward Vince and the girls gaggled around Val. Chance left to help the older folks to a nursing-home van.

Vince rested a fatherly grip on the teens' shoulders and ushered the lanky group toward the door. "Hop in the van. We'll be there in a sec. I need a word with Miss Russo alone."

Val expected Vince to lord her words over her or douse her with scorn. But instead he nodded toward Logan. "He didn't swim today. Kid loved water last week. What's his story?"

Val walked with Vince toward the glass door. The teens piled into the van outside. "I'm not sure yet. I met them barely four weeks ago." Should she mention the bruises?

"How do you know them?"

"They live in my neighborhood. I invited them to a youth bash at my house and ten or so of them showed up. Then twelve of them showed up for this swim program."

Something told her to trust Vince with her concerns

over Logan. She cleared her throat. "I'm concerned. He has fresh bruises on his arm."

"I saw that."

Vince eyed the teens in the van. "You think one of the other kids is whaling on him?"

"I don't think it's one of the kids. I overheard one of them ask Logan if he was getting into it with his mother's boyfriend again."

"That tall kid, Julio, he live in your neighborhood, too?" Concern covered his face.

"Yes. Why?"

"Because the tattoo on his wrist…?"

"Yeah?"

"It's gang-related."

"I don't think he's dangerous. But that's why I'm reaching out, Vince. To offer them an alternative."

He looked at her as though he saw her in a new light. Stared at her for a really long time, actually. Long enough that she grew nervous.

"You realize if we get proof Logan's being abused, we have to intervene," he said.

"I wouldn't think of not. I can't stand the thought of him being hurt."

"Or neglected. Which he obviously is. At least in the way of proper clothing."

She nodded.

Vince continued to run his calculating gaze over her face. "The only gangs I know of in Refuge hang out near the abandoned pavilion near the tracks."

"That's my neighborhood."

His eyes widened then narrowed. "You don't add up," he finally said as Chance approached.

Val faced Chance mostly to get out from beneath Vince's intense assessment. "We're going to the Cone Zone for pizza and ice cream. Want to join us?"

"Who?" Chance set down his camouflage duffel bag.

"Vince, the teenagers and me."

Chance looked from Val to Vince. "Really?" Surprise inflated the word.

"Yeah, real shocker." Vince viewed his watch. "So you going with?"

Chance studied them. Then grinned. "Actually, I think I'll beg off tonight."

Vince shot Chance a murderous expression. Chance picked up his duffel and, chuckling to himself, stepped away. "Catch you guys next week. Same time, same place."

Val recalled Sarah's prayer that if God intended Val to reach out to Vince, He'd provide another common ground.

Suddenly Mondays never looked so good.

Don't fall for that fellow.

Aunt Elsie's wise words from last night converged on Val's mind. She had stopped by Refuge Memorial Hospital for a visit to find Elsie in a regular room and able to sit up and talk. Val had confessed her accident to her aunt and asked Elsie to pray for Vince.

Elsie's eyes had sharpened and, between drilling

Val with questions about Vince and his heathen ways, she had unceasingly reminded Val how hard it was to live with an unbelieving spouse.

Val had balked and protested, telling Elsie she had no intentions of falling for Vince or thinking of him in a romantic manner. Just friends, she'd assured Elsie.

That's what I said about your uncle, too. Then I married him.

And though Elsie loved Uncle Parcel, Val had spent enough summers with them to know the hardship Elsie suffered with going to church alone every Sunday. Praying alone. Reading the Bible alone.

And not having the assurance even after Parcel died suddenly that her beloved husband of forty years had gone to Heaven when he'd passed.

Elsie was right. Val couldn't bear the thought of not knowing if one of her loved ones, especially her future husband or children, would be okay eternally.

Val settled her gaze on Vince but her heart on Heaven.

Don't let me fall for him.

Because, despite the bad-boy image he portrays, he's totally fall-able for.

Chapter Eight

Made no sense.

Vince hawkeyed Val at the Cone Zone three Mondays later.

And he didn't like things not making sense. Especially people. Namely a woman as complex and unpredictable as the one in front of him.

Why would a posh prosecuting attorney—and he knew she was one, too, because he'd investigated—reach out to a bunch of ragtag teens? Fringe-type kids at that.

He settled himself across from Val at a long table near the gaming section of the Cone Zone. Sixteen teens pulled out chairs and sat on either side of them with Vince and Val in the middle.

They'd come for pizza the last few Mondays after swim-safety class. Every week, Chance opted not to come. Vince suspected that was on purpose to ensure Vince had to converse more with Val.

And, not that he'd admit it to Chance, but every moment Vince was around Val, he grew more intrigued—and perplexed—by her.

She didn't match his image of most attorneys. And she certainly didn't fit the mold he'd fashioned in his mind for most Christians. She was more authentic and open. Transparent rather than pious. Inclusive rather than exclusive. Fun rather than fickle.

Her faith reminded him of that of his team leader, Joel, and their commander, Aaron Petrowski, two men Vince respected more than any others on earth.

"Miss Russo, can we play games?" one teen asked.

"Sure." She tugged a satchel out of her briefcase, pulled the strings and poured tokens onto the table.

"Cool! These for us?" He blinked in wonder at the enormous mound of game tokens.

"Have at it." She distributed a handful of tokens to each of the teens who lined up.

"Thank you!" They held out cupped hands one by one and let the next kid have a scoop until every teen had tokens. Every one of them issued hearty thanks. Impressive. Vince had noticed their manners improving in a matter of weeks of being around Val.

A handful of tokens remained on the table. The teens blinked longingly at them but didn't touch.

"We'll leave some for you guys. In case you wanna play," one girl, a born leader in Vince's eyes, said to the group, who nodded and murmured agreement.

Tokens in hand, the teens rushed in a concentrated drove toward the nearby area inside of Cone Zone, visible from where they sat. It contained pool tables, air hockey and Ping-Pong tables. An assortment of video games flashed, blinked and emitted electronic sounds. Youthy music pumped from overheard speakers.

"Those tokens cost a chunk of change," Vince said to Val.

She shrugged. "I don't mind."

All attorneys were out to take people's money. Right?

Her reaching out to the teens for no personal gain made no sense. Maybe she was being forced into community service to pay off college loans or something.

"You still paying for law school?"

She looked at him oddly. "No. I went on a scholarship."

Shot that idea down.

"Your employer making you do community service?"

"No. Why would they do that?"

Another idea shot down.

"So what gives? Why are you reaching out to those kids?"

"Because no one else is. And because I care about what happens to them."

Her words gripped him. Ripped the rug out from beneath his preconceived notions.

He recalled growing up, only a few years older

than his sister and brother, and being the only responsible person in the house.

"Where were you twenty years ago?"

She looked at him strangely and seemed to be about to ask a question. Probably looking for clarification.

The waiter came then and took their pizza and drink order.

Vince scooped up the tokens and Val's hand. "Let's go play. I want to see how good you are at air hockey."

Her cheeks flushed an attractive pink but she let him lead her to the game room.

"Ever been here after dark?" he asked her.

"No. I don't often go out after dark."

He laughed. "Why? You turn into a vampire?"

She laughed. "No, actually. I turn into a pumpkin."

He chuckled and let her hand go. Not that he really wanted to. A few of the teens watched them with curious, delighted expressions and whispers abounded.

Let them think what they may. He'd only held her hand to show her he could be a gentleman when he wanted.

"What happens here after dark?" Val asked.

"The carpet comes to life. The squiggly lines glow in the dark under black lights." He motioned above then plunked tokens in the air hockey machine.

"I'll have to come by after dark and survey it, then."

"Survey?" He rested his weight on the machine

and bit his lip from laughing at her formal word choice.

"What would a street thug say?"

"How about *check it out*?"

"Fine, I'll drop by after dark and check it out. Witness what you think is so great about it."

Vince's good mood deflated as did the giddy feeling of the lighthearted verbal sparring between them.

Witness.

Another definition of the word entered his mind. The kind that meant a witness in a court case. A bad witness.

"Witness." He felt like a zombie saying it. The word tasted like poison on his tongue as he pondered the kind of witness who perjured his brother right into the pen.

"Witness. As in watch." The concern on her face went straight through him. Reached in and touched a place no one had since he was young. He straightened, wanting for once not to turn this time into contention.

"Street lingo doesn't fit you. The kids will like you if you just be yourself."

She appeared to chew on that. "So, you're saying for me not to try so hard?"

He nodded. "I'm sayin'."

"I'd still like to learn a few informal words. I'd be a little more relatable then."

To whom? The kids? Or to him?

Vince studied her. "Okay. Lose about half of your

Purdue IQ and highfalutin words, and that'd be a start. Let's play. I'm ready to fry your bacon."

"That means?"

"Win."

"Ha-ha. We'll just see about that, oh, menacing street thug you." She grabbed the plastic sombrero-shaped mallet and pushed it expertly across the air hockey table's smooth playing surface.

Again and again, she deflected his hits toward her slot. The puck skated back and forth across thin layers of air on the rectangular game table. Of course he was letting her stay even with him.

He might even let her win. If she was lucky.

Strange since he was highly competitive.

The puck slipped through his slot, putting her ahead of him for the first time in the game. She shot him a smirk. He shot the puck in her slot. Smirked back. She put the puck almost into his slot. It bounced back to her. She slammed it hard enough it flew over the surrounding rail and off the table. It bounced and rolled across the floor.

He grinned. "Just what I thought."

"What?" Her eyebrows knitted in concentration as she watched the puck.

"You *are* competitive."

"As are you."

The puck flew back and forth across the table. No words, just the variable *clunk, clunk, clunk* of it bouncing off each end and their circular paddles.

Slam!

Bling! Blang! Bling! Blang! Bling!

"No way." Vince stared at the flashing victory lights. "Unbelievable."

She'd just won. Without his help or mercy.

"Girl, you tricked me." He set the circular blocker paddle on the table.

She laughed. "How so?"

"You distracted me. Took my mind out of the game."

Blushing, she thrust another two tokens into the machine. Then lifted her finger in the air and twirled the end of it in a circle like a tiny sword. "Touché."

He nodded, accepting her challenge. "Two out of three. Winner buys the pizza."

Her hands went to her hips. "Not fair. I already planned to pay."

The puck slipped into the retrieval slot. Vince placed it on the table and pushed it slowly toward her, giving her first shot. "Then what do you suggest?"

"Two out of three. Winner takes the loser anywhere the winner chooses. The loser must comply and stay with the winner for a two-hour span."

His brows lifted. "Even Talons?" He smirked.

"Even church?" She smirked back.

"Ouch." He raised his fingers and twirled it like a sword of his own. "Touché, mademoiselle. Touché."

Two games later, Vince scratched his forehead. They'd tied. How could they have tied?

He'd won the second game. She the first.

And the third they'd tied.

"Who ever heard of air hockey ending in a tie?" She shook her head at the machine.

"So this means?" he asked, already knowing he wouldn't like her answer.

"We both get to lead the other to a place of our choosing." Her face squirmed. "Even Talons."

He grinned. "I have a better idea. Three out of five games. Because I have no intention of going to church."

He had no intentions of taking her back to Talons either. But he'd let her squirm a little on that count.

What he did want to do was take her on the road for a long motorcycle ride along southern Illinois terrain. Over winding, wildflower-lined roads. Past soybean and cornfields. With the sun on their backs and the wind in their faces. Full-throttle. Freedom.

The thought of her arms being around him for two hours solid caused him to dig deep for more tokens.

He definitely wanted to win.

"Whoops. Looks like this game will stand." She set the puck in the final resting slot.

Vince stood. "Why?"

She gestured toward the table. "Pizza's here."

Vince came around to her. "I'm not going to church."

She whirled gracefully, sending him a maddening grin. "Oh, so you're going back on your word?"

His jaw clenched. His mind grappled. "I won't

make you go to Talons if you don't make me go to church."

She motioned the teens over. "Actually, Talons has great barbecue ribs."

"You're even more stubborn than I thought." He shook his head. "Remind me never to go up against you in a court of law." He helped herd the gangly teens.

Val was still laughing when she settled in her seat.

He pushed her forward and leaned in, close to her ear. "And for the record, I never go back on my word."

She smirked and unfolded her silverware. "I know."

He served her, then the teens. Val watched him carefully.

"What?" His ears heated at her gentle but direct perusal.

"You surprise me sometimes, is all."

"Yeah? Makes two of us."

Dead silence descended as Val bowed her head and prayed over the meal.

The teens blinked at each other but seemed at ease, so they'd obviously grown accustomed to her doing it.

Not Vince. He froze in place, not knowing what to do or say.

Scary thing was, the teens looked to him. He could read the questions in their eyes. Like, *why didn't you pray?*

He hoped he never had to answer that.

"You eat pizza with a fork? All properlike?" Vince dipped his forehead toward Val's plate.

She eyed her nicely cut-up pizza and dabbed her mouth before speaking. "Yes. And I don't put my elbows on the table either."

He looked sideways at her. "What's wrong with elbows on a table?"

She laughed. "You teach me urban texting and gang-related rhetoric, and I'll teach you formal restaurant and social etiquette."

"Rhetoric? You mean street slang?"

"See?" She patted his hand. "You're teaching me already."

After homemade cantaloupe ice cream, for which Cone Zone was famous, the teens piled into the van while Vince and Val sparred over who'd pay for the pizza and dessert.

"I might seem like a jerk but I never let a lady pay."

"You did at Talons."

He grinned. "I didn't think you were a lady then."

She laughed out loud. "What did you think I was?"

"The first word that comes to mind wouldn't be proper to say in front of minors. But suffice it to say I thought you were an attorney."

"Which I am."

"But you don't act like one."

She studied him carefully and her face softened. Almost into pity. The absolute last thing he wanted to see reflecting in her eyes. So why was it there? She didn't know about his brother, right? How could she?

"Besides, I lied." Vince slapped a hundred-dollar bill in front of the register.

"About?" Val finally gave up and put her wallet away.

"Talons. I paid your tab. Not Chance."

That made her momentarily lost for words. His mind scrambled. How to keep conversation going? He liked to watch the way her face openly expressed emotion and how vividly her eyes lit up when she listened. Not to mention he liked listening to the sound of her voice and all that jazz.

"So," he said, nodding to the group of teens waiting for the others to come out of the bathroom. "Why is it the girls wear jeans three sizes too small and the boys ten sizes too big?"

Val laughed. "Style, I guess."

A few straggling kids meandered close to Vince and Val. "Don't you hate it when you date a guy who's just insanely pimpled and nerdy? Then when you break up with them they get insanely hot?" one of the girls said to another, eyeing a boy exiting a car outside.

Vince glanced at Val and laughed. She smiled and shook her head. "To be young again."

"You're still young."

She shrugged. "At heart."

"Hey, you look good. You're certainly no old maid. People aren't old until they hit triple digits."

"Yeah. Well, I'm turning thirty next month."

"Thirty. Wow. You *are* old."

She smacked him.

"So, what's wrong with thirty?" Vince held open the door for her.

"Nothing's especially wrong with thirty. But, thirty *and still single* is misery."

"Ah. The family type."

"Yeah. I envisioned myself married with children by now."

"So what's the problem?"

She laughed. "You tell me. I guess I just attract the wrong kind of guy."

"And what's the wrong kind of guy for you?"

"The kind who can't fully commit. At least not to one girl. And the kind of guy who can't commit to God and share my faith."

He studied her carefully. "Wow. If I'm counting right, that's at least four strikes against me. So remind yourself never to fall for me."

Her countenance fell.

Made him feel like a total jerk.

She quickly covered her expression. "I'd never fall for you."

"Yee-ouch. Brutal. I think I might be offended."

She laughed and motioned the teens finally coming out of the bathroom toward the exit they waited by. "I doubt it. I could never see you with an attorney."

"Or with a Christian."

"Or with someone who doesn't particularly care for motorcycles. Or that kind of lifestyle."

"Or with someone who can't bring herself to let her elbows rest on a table."

"Yeah. We'd never match."

"Never." Vince held open the door, wondering two things. One, why the world looked so bleak all of a sudden. And two, why Val looked the same.

"Whoa, they're going nutso." She swooshed spiky tendrils of bangs across her forehead as she watched the teens running down the van aisle. He walked beside her to curb the chaos mounting inside the van.

Once in the front passenger seat, Vince dialed down the music and faced the back. "You guys sure you want her driving?"

Val shushed him. "You're never going to let me live that down."

"Never." He clicked his seat belt.

Val rolled her eyes and backed out.

"Why you say that, bro?" Julio asked.

"No reason." Vince winked at Val. Decided he wouldn't share information about the crash that caused them to meet.

Suddenly the crash didn't seem all that bad.

Until images of his brother collided with the feel-good emotion being with Val evoked. Remnants of his brother's handiwork scattered like thrown-away litter in the road.

He shoved the pleasantness of being in her presence aside.

He could not, would not, befriend the Enemy.

She might bring a little interest into a boring season of his life.

But nothing she could do could bring back his bike.

Or his brother.

So her mission was useless. He might befriend her for a while to ease her discomfort. And she might try to convert him though she claimed she wouldn't.

If he ignored her, she'd eventually go away. Just like his mom had when his dad neglected her.

If Vince ignored thoughts of Val that kept on him like rubber to a road, they'd eventually go away.

Right?

These thoughts and feelings he got when he was around her. Crazy stuff. The way he couldn't stop thinking about her. How intelligent and warm and caring she was.

Totally not his type. A woman like that?

She deserved far better.

He'd avoid her at all costs. No matter the knot that the thought of doing so stuck in his throat.

He'd resist and evade her, and she'd eventually give up.

Chapter Nine

"I refuse to give up," Val said on the phone to Sarah who'd suggested she drop by the DZ to see Vince.

"He hasn't called?"

"No. Nor was he at the pool yesterday or the Monday before or the Monday before that."

"I'll bet he switched places with a teammate."

"Yeah, Brockton. Thanks for talking me through the nervousness, Sarah. I never know how Vince is going to respond."

"I'm glad you called me."

Seeing Logan becoming increasingly distressed, Val resorted to phoning Sarah, who assured her that Vince always worked at the DZ on Tuesdays.

So here she was in her newly repaired car, driving down Peña's Landing toward the facility which housed the man who could be Logan's hope.

"Logan deflected my attempts at communication.

He said he'd talk to Vince and no one else." Would Vince open up and offer Logan that hope?

"Let me pray for you guys," Sarah said. "Lord, there's a reason beyond what we know that you can see about why Logan feels a kinship with Vince. Help Vince see that, too."

"And help him to reach out of the ashes of his own past and pain to help Logan before it's too late."

"Amen," Sarah whispered.

"I'm here."

She pulled into the far end of the DZ's vast parking area. She surveyed the section of lot nearest the building.

There. The motorcycle she knew to be Vince's because she'd seen him ride it to the pool. "He's here. Please pray. I feel like I'm headed to trial."

"I will. Give him time, Val. He'll come around."

"Thanks. I appreciate that. Talk to you Thursday."

"Yes. I'm looking forward to it." They'd agreed to meet at Square Beans, a coffee and pastry shop on the town square, which was really a circle.

Val hung up feeling thankful for her friendship with Sarah, who was set to wed Aaron in a matter of weeks.

Her stomach performed a series of flips as she eyed the DZ pole barn and brick-fronted structure. It appeared as hard and as formidable as Vince.

This wasn't about her any longer. The teens had been asking for him. Especially Logan.

For Logan, she'd gird her courage and face Vince.

Even his blatant rejection of her attempts at friendship.

She walked across the asphalt and entered the DZ facility. Chance looked up from where he stood behind the counter. His eyes veered toward the right wall, lined with doors. Then back.

Val pivoted that way in time to see Vince slithering into what looked like a utility closet.

Chance shuffled papers nervously.

Hand on her hip, she trucked to the counter. "I need to talk to him. It's important."

Chance pulled his lip between his teeth and tried to look dumb.

"C'mon, Chance. It's not about me. I'm concerned about one of the teens. Logan. He's asking for Vince."

Chance's eyes darted to the closet. Then back to Val. "I don't know. If he's here, he might be in a sour mood."

"If? I know he's here. If you won't let me talk to Vince, then at least give him the message about Logan."

Joel came up. "Where's Reardon?" he asked Chance.

Chance eyed the closet. "Uh, well, he's around."

"And where is 'around'?"

"Uh, he could be in the supply closet."

Joel stared at Chance. Then eyed Val. Then the closet where zero signs of activity originated.

Joel raised his hands. "Never mind. I don't want to know." He walked off shaking his head.

"Fine. Go," Chance said low to Val and nodded toward the closet. "But don't dare tell him I told you where his hiding place is."

She laughed. "I saw him tuck tail and run in there when I came in anyway."

Once at the closet, Val jerked open the door.

Vince, standing between a mop bucket and a row of neon-colored jackets, gave a slight jerk and blinked at the intrusive light. He had that "caught" look in his eyes.

"Since when are you a coward, bad boy?" Val stepped into the closet, which grew much smaller now that she was in there. Alone with bad boy. But, for Logan, she wouldn't flinch or back down until she had results. Even a no. Regardless of Vince's resistance tactics, she'd try.

"Since you started stalking me." He grinned. "Although, normally I wouldn't complain about a woman calling me every ten minutes."

"I only call once a day."

He folded arms across his very wide, well-developed chest. Melded nicely into muscled shoulders and strenuously cut arms. She tore away her gaze when he flexed his biceps, alerting her that he noticed her noticing his physique.

"Okay, fine. I call twice daily. Once to here and once at your house."

He raised his chin in what she knew to be his intimidation stance. Guess what? It worked.

Her heart pounded heat into her face. Especially when he didn't speak for several beats. Just scowled at her.

"How'd you get my home number?" he finally pushed through teeth he'd pressed together.

She shrugged and avoided his gaze.

Vince slid caustic looks over her shoulder through the crack in the door at the counter where Chance helped a skydiving patron. "Probably the same rat fink way you learned I was in this closet."

"Don't blame Chance. He's not the source. I got your number from Logan. He said you gave it to him. But he's afraid to call you first."

"Wow. You wanted to find me bad enough you'd coerce a troubled kid for my number?" A faux dreamy look entered his eyes. "Last time I was in a closet alone with a desperate girl was in junior high. Want to know what we were doing in there?"

Her face heated. "I most certainly do not."

"How about I show you, then?" He reached for her and made mock smooching sounds with his lips.

His mouth was pure flirtation. But his eyes held total mockery.

Wasn't working. Well, the flirtation part anyway. Mostly because she knew he wasn't serious. Not about her.

She smacked his arm. "Vince, be real."

"I am." He tugged her close. Heat. The man was a lady toaster! "Come closer, baby."

Had he meant it, she might actually have melted.

"I'm here about Logan."

He stilled. Leaned back. Tilted his head in listen mode.

"Something bad is going on at home. Said he didn't feel like he could talk to me. He's asking for you."

Even in the dim closet, she could see concern fill eyes that her words had severely sobered. Compassion trickled into his expression, softening his face, causing the immovable hardness to recede from his eyes.

Then, out-of-nowhere anger lashed from those eyes and, without warning, he surged toward her.

She ducked and nearly cowered into a ball until she realized he'd only moved past her to press his ear against the door. Eyes flashing magma, he shoved it open.

Surprised grunts, then scuffling and scrambling on the other side of the pushed-open door made Val realize half of Vince's team had been up against it eavesdropping on them.

The thought made her want to laugh.

Especially when Vince issued each of them annihilating looks. She pressed a hand against her mouth but a high-pitched giggle escaped.

He turned his fiery gaze on her, too, then.

Only made her want to laugh more. She shoved knuckles into her mouth but could barely contain it. Air built up in her chest from the effort and a bugling wheeze burst out. His jaw clenched. His gaze dropped to her shoulders which would not stop jerking from the uncontainable laugh.

Vince, still firing irritated glances at his scrambling, snickering team, waved her sharply toward tables farthest away from his teammates in the corner of the room. The madder he got the more she wanted to laugh.

Only thoughts of Logan and concern for his situation sobered her back to a point of seriousness.

"About Logan. What do we do?" Vince asked, once seated. All irritation fled his face and sincerity took its place.

"I'm pretty sure there's a domestic violence issue going on between Logan and his mom's boyfriend."

"How do you know?" Deep concern lined his tone.

"Some of the kids came to me with information. Privately. One on one, not knowing the others had also come in confidence with similar stories. Things they hear and see."

"Wow. This is heavy." Vince raked a hand over his head, which was shaved Mohawk-ish above his ears yet buzzed on top. His hair was blacker than the darkest night she'd ever seen. His eyes, too. A woman could melt in their richness.

He leaned forward. "Be careful. You'll bump your chin." Humor glimmered in his eyes.

Face aflame, she cleared her throat and sat up straight, realizing she'd somehow slid down in her chair. Way down. "They're very concerned."

"As they should be. Why'd they tell you?"

"Not sure. I guess they thought they could trust me."

"Because you reached out when no one else would." Something distant entered his words. An echo resided in his eyes. Something she couldn't pinpoint. "Did you ask Logan?"

"I tried. But he seemed uncomfortable. Said he'd rather talk to you. He asked when you'd be back. Gave me your number. Asked me to call you."

He waved a dismissing hand. "Yeah, well, sorry."

"You've been avoiding me on purpose?"

Silence.

"Vince?"

He rubbed his strong chin and didn't answer.

She tried not to stare but she couldn't help it. Since when did tall, dark and brooding attract her? Especially since his brooding was accompanied by a strikingly short fuse in the way of tempers.

After a moment of what seemed to be intense thinking, Vince leaned forward. "That's not important now. What's important is Logan."

She inhaled deeply, not wanting to say this but willing for Logan. "Vince, if you promise to reach out to him, I'll promise to leave you alone."

He blinked, then leveled her with a look. "I don't need to be convinced."

"So you want to help him?" She took hold of his hand. Squeezed. "Because you're meant to. I know it with everything in me. You were created to do this. Reach them. Kids like Logan."

Her words looked to both conflict and pierce him. Like he wanted to embrace the concept and fight it at the same time. He didn't speak for the longest moments.

Then his gaze drifted to her hand, still firmly holding his. If only she could impart mercy through osmosis. She strengthened her grip.

But when his tense hand loosened and his fingertip brushed a lazy trail underneath the sensitive skin of her palm, she realized mercy was the last thing either felt at the moment.

She jerked her hand back, surprised at how powerful that one small touch from the tip of his finger was. "What are you doing? Checking my pulse?"

He leaned in and his eyes darkened to an unmistakable shade of knowing. "I don't need to check your pulse to know the effect I have on you." His voice grew low and gruff.

She gritted her teeth. Mostly because he was right. "Vince, please. Focus on Logan."

He pulled back. Eyed her hand that had held his. "Don't touch me like that again. Not unless you can own up to it."

She did not. Did not. Did not *even* want to ponder his meaning. Especially since something told her that this time he wasn't kidding. She'd reached something in him. An emotional core that he didn't want tapped.

She huffed, hoping to diffuse this weirdness,

unravel romantic threads trying to weave between them. But like him, the thread was strong and stubborn. Too hard to break?

If the answer was yes, her "pity project" was done. Over. If she couldn't stay on emotional track, hold her attraction at bay and keep her feelings intact, she'd have to back away. The thought withered her with disappointment.

Oh, Lord. Is my heart already hemmed in stitches?

If so, the parting would be ever more painful.

"You don't affect me like that," she blurted.

His eyes gave off that "get real" gleam. "Don't kid yourself."

Because he was serious, she was too stunned to speak.

"Logan." He pulled out his phone. "How do I find him?"

She fiddled with her pocketbook. The new one she'd picked up at the Harley shop. First time she'd ventured in. Why she'd purchased a wallet she thought Vince would like she had no idea. Embroiled. That's what she was becoming.

She straightened her spine the way she did before heading into a courtroom to do battle. "He said not to call. He promised to be at the pool next Monday. Will you?"

"I'll be there. For Logan." He stood, putting emphasis on Logan. Something had gone cold in his eyes.

"For what it's worth, I've missed you on Mondays."

Irritation flashed in his eyes. "It's worth nothing, lady. Look, I need to get back to work."

Disappointment clogged her throat.

Hope plummeted inside her.

He was shutting her out.

Her hand tingled where remnants of his earlier touch remained. How badly she wanted to get through to him. To connect. Not physically. But emotionally. Spiritually.

To reach and reverse the hurt in his soul.

God, help me please. I'm sinking faster than I can swim. How did I come to care about him so?

She swallowed sadness back and rose, gesturing toward the utility room he'd hidden in. "Back to work you go…cleaning out the closet? Finding skeletons maybe?"

His steps hitched and he looked like he could laugh but then he angled his face away from her and continued on. So she wouldn't see.

Too late.

She'd caught the wounded look in his eyes, the same as the day of the wreck.

The same look she'd seen in Logan's eyes last night at the pool when Vince never walked through the doors.

Outside, she'd almost reached her car when rapid footsteps echoed on the lot. At her door now, she turned.

Vince, halfway across, waved a restraining hand. "Wait up," he called, sprinting toward her.

She nodded yet slid into her car, fearing her reaction if he pulled her into his arms. Because he looked for once like he could.

Then fear struck that he'd changed his mind about reaching out to Logan. The despair in that thought made her want to unleash angry tears. For Logan. And for Vince.

Because by reaching out, she knew that God was reaching in. And that somehow Logan would be as healing to Vince as Vince would be to Logan.

If he'd only reach out. She stared into his eyes as he ran. *Reach, Vince. Take the hand and the plan that God has offered.*

Car started, she rolled her window down halfway as he approached, breathless. Head bent, his hands slid to his knees and he caught his breath.

"Please don't tell me you've changed your mind."

"Told you, I never go back on my word. Which is why I'm here." Straightening, he shuffled from foot to foot.

She turned off her ignition, knowing instinctively that what he was about to say was incredibly hard for him.

He white-knuckled the window. "I mean, we had a deal, right? You and me. I take you somewhere and you—you—you—"

Joy erupted. "Take you to church."

He scowled. "Something like that."

She studied him a moment. "You're not ready."

Confusion blinked across his eyes. "What?"

She restarted her car. "Coercion tactics never work. You're not ready to go to church."

Now he looked miffed. "I'm not scared the walls are gonna cave in on me if that's what you think."

She laughed. "That's not what I think. But I know you're not ready. And frankly, I'm not ready to return to Talons."

His face softened. "I hadn't really planned to take you back. There, I mean. Take you back there." He cleared his throat.

"Really?"

"Really."

She rested her hands on the steering wheel and examined his face.

He raked a hand along his sturdy neck and tilted his well-defined shoulders in pacing maneuvers. "Look. This is hard for me to say. To admit. But, I—" He blew an eternal breath. "With you, I— It's like this. I feel good when I'm around you. You make me think about stuff. Good stuff. God stuff. And, well, I'm not gonna lie. You're hot—I—mean, attractive. And yeah, I like you *that* way. But, I value our friendship more."

She studied his twitchy gestures. Imagine, Mr. Tall, Dark and Titanium, nervous.

"I believe you, Vince."

He blew out a relieved breath. "Good. That's good."

"So, I'm curious. If not Talons, where did you

plan to take me?" If the destination was more hard-core than Talons, she was scared to know the answer.

"For a ride."

"A ride." *That's it? That can't be it.* "Literal or figurative?"

"What?"

"What kind?"

"On my bike. Literal."

"You mean that two-wheeled death trap that you call a motorcycle?"

"It's only a death trap when sizzling-red sedans scream through red lights and race across oncoming traffic to smash into it."

Gulp. "Good point."

He grinned wide. And it caused her heart to flutter so ridiculously hard that the guys, faces smooshed to stare out the far DZ windows at them, probably noticed.

"But since the biggest danger to us seems to be you, and you'll be on the back of the bike with me instead of coming directly at me in a wet, busy intersection, I think we'll be pretty safe."

Her hands loosened. "I've never ridden. I might be nervous."

"I'll teach you how to hold on. Keep you safe. Nothing bad will happen. Promise."

Somehow she knew his promise carried meaning beyond the bike ride. He wanted purity to rule their friendship.

"C'mon, Val. Go riding with me. Please?"

For once his teasing faded and his words sounded sincere, hopeful even. When she didn't answer right away, an uncharacteristic vulnerability entered his hard eyes.

Reminded her of the fear she'd had that he'd reject her plea to reach out to Logan.

By asking her to go for a ride with him, to enter his turf, he had recognized her reaching out to him. And he was reaching back. Finally reaching back.

He'd said she made him think about God things. And she knew with certainty he wasn't carroting her along.

No way could she bail on their friendship now.

If she wanted to earn his trust, she had to extend her own.

"I'd love to go riding with you, Vince. Name the time and I'll be ready."

Chapter Ten

"Insanity must be closing in. I'm actually looking forward to lunch with this dame."

Chance chuckled. Vince went to the mirror and checked his appearance once more. Checked the clock.

"Time to go."

He stepped outside their B and B unit and climbed on his bike. Chance fastened the extra helmet to the saddlebag. Vince revved the gas until the power vibrated his being.

The only thing he loved more than motorcycle-riding was skydiving.

Maybe he'd talk her into doing that with him, too.

Strange, this shift. This want to be with her. Feelings of looking forward to talking to her. Even about God stuff. Especially about God stuff. Little strange blips in his chest when her number showed up on caller ID, even times he refused to let himself answer. Let himself hope.

You're no good for her.

So why did being with her feel so good?

"Be careful." Chance waved.

Vince maneuvered the bike out of his driveway and onto the street. He accelerated, popping a wheelie. Of course he wouldn't do that with her on back, so he needed to get it out of his system now.

The daredevil in him took over and he popped three more wheelies before reaching the end of the road.

He stopped to fuel up at a gas station and double-checked the address she'd given him. Reluctantly given, he might add. Like she hadn't wanted him to know where she lived. He'd assumed because of safety reasons.

Like she didn't fully trust him.

Which bugged him more than he wanted to admit.

Ten minutes later, Vince passed the residence three times to confirm the address.

He stared at the house. Disbelief coursed through him. He double-checked the address on the phone then on the paper.

"My motorcycle shed is nicer than this home."

This can't be it.

Vince stared at the tiny structure with the tilted numbers on the faded front door. He reread the paper. Sure enough, identical address.

This was her home? Couldn't be. Surely a big-city attorney would live in a larger, nicer house?

The riffraff hanging on the corner slammed his

body into high alert. Steel bars gleamed on surrounding establishment windows—not a great sign the area was safe. He must have transcribed her address wrong.

When he turned to go, the front door creaked open. "Vince?"

He turned at her voice. She looked unsure as she stepped out onto the second step because the top one was crumbling. He walked back toward the house.

A quick assessment of her told him two things. One, she was nervous as all get out, and two, she'd taken extraordinary care to fix herself up.

Oorah!

Gone was the professional updo that pulled her face too tight. Her hair lay in the same short, wispy angles it had the day of the wreck. Kind of wild. Kind of elfish.

A warm, nervous smile coated in light pink lipstick took the place of her usual formally compressed lips and poised, rigid stance.

Color brightened her cheeks and even bolder color coated her smoky eyes, making her look less severe, less maidenly, more womanly. Well, less lawyerly.

His gaze skimmed her halter-style shirt-skirt that accentuated tanned, toned arms. Looked like an above-the-knees sundress. Stylish, lacy-bottomed leotard things modestly brushed her ankles. Platform, jeweled sandals, flip-flop style with shiny gold gladiator-looking straps revealed tanned feet with nail polish the color of her lips. Her toes curled and her chin lowered, letting him know she grew uncomfortable with his outright scrutiny.

"Nice getup," he said, not knowing any other way to give a compliment to a lady. She'd probably deck him if he called her some of the edgy terms he'd charm his biker-babe dates with. Not that this was a date. Really.

Now, how to tell her that flip-flops and dresses were a bad idea on a bike? Too easy to get legs burned on the exhaust or gravel should he accidentally spill the bike.

She smiled and tucked an errant curl behind her ear. "Thank you." Her face pulled a slight contortion. "I think." She shut her door then shoved a key through the slot and turned. In a neighborhood like this, he was glad she had sense enough to know to keep her doors locked.

He scratched his forehead. "Uh, you look great. But…"

Wordlessly she paused.

How to say this? "Trust me. You've got great legs. Perfect for skirts. But, I'd rather you wear jeans. Heavy ones that cling to your ankles. Not too flared." Too easy to get snagged. "Like that newish pair you wore on the fifth youth trip to Cone Zone with the frilly-sleeved white pirate-looking shirt. Those would do."

Her mouth fell open. She blinked slowly.

"I—er, not that I'd *rather* you wear jeans. It's just—jeans are *safer* on a bike. Besides, the wind, it can be brutally cold on the open highway."

Her face righted itself. "Ah. Got it. I'll just be a minute." She started back inside then paused at her open door. "Would you like to come in?"

Boy, would he.

He took three fast steps back. "No, ma'am."

Looked way too cozy in there.

She tilted her face and stared at him oddly.

Which was when he realized sweat beads were breaking out over his forehead. His throat felt like sandpaper.

What on earth was wrong with him?

He never got nervous on dates. Never.

Not that this was a date-date. A friendship outing. Yeah. That's what this was.

Don't forget it.

He motioned her on. "You go right ahead."

She nodded and proceeded in.

Vince yanked out a bandanna and swiped his face. "It's all her fault. She's distracting." Why, he hadn't so much as looked at another woman since meeting her.

Freaky odd.

Even odder, for the first time ever in his life, he actually *wanted* his mind and imagination to keep her out of their gutters.

Moments later she peeked her head out. "Should I wear socks, too?"

He nodded. And averted his gaze.

Good as those jeans and that fun-but-feminine shirt looked, he wished she'd stick to sensible and wear a suit of armor.

He yanked out his hanky again and swiped sweat beads off the back of his neck and wished for once he was a praying man. He could use mental help about now.

"Hey, bring a jacket. We might be out late," he called as she rummaged around in her front closet near the doorway.

Brock would never believe in a million years how nervous Val made Vince.

He forced himself to calm down by staring at the lustrous sky, which was the only thing that could compete with a well-built woman as far as keeping his attention went.

She leaned out. "Where are you taking me?"

"It's a surprise," he hedged, trying to find curvy shapes in the clouds. It helped that tails of white jet streams formed what appeared to be three crosses in the super-blue sky.

Thanks for that.

The spontaneity of his thoughts freaked him out.

Val reappeared. "Great! I love adventures and surprises." Excitement crackled in her sentence. She did a little hop. He almost laughed.

Maybe he wouldn't tell her that their destination was a surprise mainly because he didn't exactly plan that far ahead. He was more of a spontaneous kind of guy, whereas he imagined she was a planner.

Yet another reason to keep an emotional distance. Something that, the more he'd gotten to know her,

her heart of compassion especially where Logan was concerned, was becoming increasingly difficult.

He plucked the helmet he'd bought especially for her from its holder on his bike. Ridiculous that it had taken him a solid hour to pick it out. He'd finally gotten a female employee at Refuge's Harley Davidson shop to help him out with choosing Val's helmet.

No man in his right mind would spend an hour shopping for a single item in a store. Unless it was a tool shop or an electronics outlet.

Why he'd angsted so long and hard over a helmet perplexed him as much as the process of picking the perfect one. What she thought mattered. She might only wear the costly thing once. But he wanted that once to be special.

Well, it's not like protective headgear was meant to be a fashion statement anyway. Well, maybe this one was.

As he held the glittery blue helmet and let the weight of its true purpose sink in, a streak of uncharacteristic fear went through him.

What if it didn't fit?

What if someone like her crashed into them and harmed her?

He'd promised to keep her safe.

What if he didn't deliver?

He knew the hard way that life and death rarely resided within human control.

Vince's palms grew sweaty. He knew he was a great driver, but he couldn't control other drivers. And taking her life into his hands made him uneasy.

Why?

Never before had risking his life for others bothered him. Yet this wasn't a rescue mission.

This was a friendly bike ride.

That bothered him more than it ought. After all, his military mantra was that he had nothing to fear except fear itself. Well, that and giant spiders.

Especially Middle Eastern ones that rivaled the size of his palm and liked to crawl in and share his desert-camouflage sleeping bag without prior clearance.

But not even foreign spiders could compete with this sudden, unexplained unease about their bike ride.

For a second time he wished he was a praying man.

Because if he were, he'd ask the Big Guy to keep them safe so she could enjoy the thrill of the ride.

A strange sensation went through him. Why didn't he just ask?

Would anyone listen if he did?

For the first time he felt someone might.

She reemerged wearing proper riding gear. "You okay?"

He jerked. "Yeah, why?"

"You look a little pale."

"Nah. I'm fine."

His palms moistened as he considered the road.

The traffic. Every dangerous scenario went through his mind.

"Vince?" She approached, concern evident.

And suddenly he knew that somehow, despite his walls and her faith and all odds stacked against them, he'd come to care deeply about her.

She eyed the bike and clasped her hands together in an anticipatory motion. "I hope this outfit is okay. Ready?"

She waited.

He studied her. And listened with his whole heart.

Something shifted inside him. He wanted more than anything to be able to ask God to protect her. But he couldn't make his mouth work.

Not after God never heard him the first time.

He forced his mind to think of the God he knew from childhood.

Reached deep.

For the faith that he'd once held that God would not only hear but answer his prayers.

Another something shifted inside.

And for the first time since he was a boy, he felt a pinhole of breakthrough between him and heaven.

Like an open line, as small as fishing wire but there. The lifeline that had been his prayer life before life's brutality disillusioned it.

Tsunamis of relief, relief like he'd never known, rushed through that pinhole, tearing it, breaking it, opening. Wider.

Something pushed through.

A granule of faith?

His mind released the words that he couldn't yet bring himself to say out loud.

Keep her safe.

"Ready?" she repeated, watching him like a sniper to his scope.

I am now.

He handed her the helmet. "Ready."

She placed it on her head.

He helped her adjust the chin straps. His knuckles brushing against her skin seared his flesh.

God help me.

He was dangerously attracted to her.

I'm no good for her. You know I'm no good. Protect her. Yes. Even from me.

Especially from me.

Her greatest danger wasn't in the road. Not if he never changed.

"I want to."

She whirled. "What?"

He shook his head. Both to deflect her question and to shake the shock that he'd actually said the prayer with his mouth rather than with his mind.

Thanks.

Relief rushed through him that the prayer-thought slipped out infinitely easier this time.

"Vince?" Her voice sounded different somehow.

He chanced a look at her and found her still watching him intently.

Like she'd noticed the shift and sensed the epic battle, but couldn't define or align it.

"Feeling okay today?" She rested her hand on his forearm.

He stared at her hands. Wanted to hold them again. Hold her. And not let go this time.

"Yeah. I'm all right. Never better, in fact." He motioned toward the bike.

"How long you plan to live here?" Vince asked as they stepped from the yard toward the gravel driveway where he'd parked his bike.

"As long as I can."

He scoped the neighborhood. "You ought to find a safer area."

She didn't answer except to cast a thoughtful expression his way.

He gestured toward his motorcycle. "Nice day for a ride."

She lifted her purse strap over her shoulder. A purse that suddenly looked familiar.

Where'd he seen one like it before?

It hit him then.

"New purse?"

She blushed. "Yes."

"Did you get it at the Harley shop? Because it looks like one of their custom-made ones."

She cleared her throat and stuffed her wallet under her arm. Almost like hiding it. "Yes. In fact, I did."

He grinned. "You went in there?"

She loosed a scowl. "Why wouldn't I?"

He grinned wider and shrugged.

She lowered her chin and bit her lip. "Did you purchase another bike?"

He forced his face to stay neutral. "Nah. This is my old ride. You might want to leave that here," he said of her wallet-purse. "All you really need is ID."

She nodded slowly and neared her car. She unlocked the trunk and stuck her purse inside. The trunk door shut with a *clunk.*

She handed him her license on the way to the bike. "I'm not sure where to put my money."

"You really won't need it."

She fisted the fifty and handed it over to him.

He laughed. "I won't steal your cash, counselor."

She tilted her head. "Very funny. You *really* don't like attorneys, do you?"

He snorted. "You *really* don't want me to answer that."

"Vince, I'm sorry about your—" She shook her head as though to curb her words. For a moment she looked ready to say something else—then stopped herself.

What had she been about to say?

She was sorry about his *what?*

Feeling things had dampened between them, he scrambled for something worthwhile to say.

"You know, I've heard that women who paint their toenails are ninety per cent less likely to commit suicide than women who don't."

Her head whipped up and her facial expression confirmed shock at the subject matter. But quickly she subdued it with a considerate expression. "Oh. That makes sense, I suppose."

He wished he were better at conversation with a lady.

But this wasn't like a real date. They both just needed to get stuff off their chests. "Listen, let's face it. We've been brought in each other's paths for a reason."

Her eyebrows lowered. "Sounds as though you *do* believe in a higher power. Otherwise what reason would there be for any reason?"

What could he say to that? Certainly couldn't refute it. It scared him how easily she made him ponder things of God.

Time to change the old subject.

"I expected someone like you to live in a posh gated community or something."

She froze. "I think I'm offended. You're stereotyping me. I don't like it."

He laughed and scooted forward on the seat so she could fit behind him. She did. And it was snug. He liked it. This was going to be some ride.

He kicked the stand up and fired up the engine. Her hands instantly came up to clutch his shoulders.

He grinned.

Yep. Some ride.

He revved the engine until he could feel the vibrations nearly to his bone. Her fingernails dug into his shoulders. He laughed.

She smacked his back. "You're doing that on purpose."

He nodded. "Hold on!" he said above the engine noise.

Kicked it into gear and they were off. An endearing shriek that ended in a giggle came out of her and her hands flew from his shoulders to snake around his waist.

Ah! Bliss.

The cool wind in his face and a warm woman against his back.

The only woman he could envision wanting at his side for life. Vince revved the engine.

For today, he'd pretend she was his.

For by nightfall, he'd have to give her back to the God he knew loved her enough to protect her.

From him.

Chapter Eleven

"**Y**ou're feeling safer," Vince said to Val on their third bike ride and picnic in as many days. "More comfortable on the bike." Settled on the camouflage blanket beside her, he plucked a grape out of the basket resting between them.

"Much." Park-goers milled around on bikes or walking tracks. Squirrels scurried about looking for lost morsels. Birds fluttered from tree to blooming tree chirping and carrying on. Reminded her to pick millet up for Elsie's bird. They'd be moving in with Val temporarily so Elsie could continue physical rehab in Refuge.

She smoothed wrinkles out of the blanket and stretched out on her side. "How did you know?"

"For one thing you don't puncture my ribs with your fingernails anymore. For another, you don't ride so rigid when we go down the road."

"Because southern Illinois thankfully has gentle curves on most roads."

"That's because cars generally careen off them if curves are too sharp."

She laughed. "Who knew it could be so fun?"

He tossed an acorn at her. "Me."

She tossed the acorn back. He caught it without looking. His speed, skill and agility floored her.

"If you are as adept flying your military parachute as you are handling the bike and all those teens at the pool, I hope the people your team risks their lives to rescue know how blessed they are."

His smile faded. "Blessed? That's not a word you should use in the same sentence with anything remotely related to me."

"Why not?"

"Because it implies I'm some kinda answer to someone's prayers." A scowl furrowed his brows.

"Maybe you are. I'm sure you have been, in fact."

"Whatever. You just go on believing your nice little utopian illusion." He threw an acorn up in the air. When it came back down, he caught then crushed it in his grip.

Wow. He really didn't like discussing things of God.

"Why are you afraid?" Val rolled onto her stomach, glad for soft, newly sprouted grass. She propped herself up with her fist and watched park visitors stroll by.

"Of?" Vince, four feet away with arms folded behind his head as he lay on his back, kept staring at the sky.

"Committing your heart to Him."

"Because I don't devote half-heartedly or do things halfway. If I'm gonna party, I'm gonna party my brains out. If I'm gonna serve God, I'm gonna go for the gusto. But I won't do both simultaneously." He rolled over to face her.

"You have the right idea about devotion, Vince. But know you don't have to come clean before coming to Him."

His lazy gaze suggested he may or may not have heard or taken seriously what she said. He plucked a dandelion out of the grass and, mesmerizingly slow, stretched it toward her. She reached to take it. He tugged it back.

Then he covered her hand with his. "Close your eyes."

Since they were surrounded by people, she obliged, even though he had an ornery look about him.

A second after her eyes closed, a light, brushing sensation traveled along her cheekbone. Across her jawline. Up the other side of her face. Above her eyebrow. Across her forehead. Down her nose.

She fluttered her eyes open. "I could be hypnotized by that."

He smiled. And handed her the flower, which she suddenly realized was no flower.

But a bracelet with several charms dangling from it.

She sat up, pulse accelerating. "For me?"

He nodded. Placed it in her hand.

"But it felt like dandelion fuzz." She brushed the

side of her face. How on earth could a tough man's touch be so tender?

He grinned. And pulled his other hand from behind his back.

She laughed. "The dandelion. So which one were you tickling my face with?"

"What do you think?" He smiled. And handed her the flower.

Eyes closed, she brushed it across her skin. Then the bracelet. "I don't know. The metal is warm from being cradled in your hand. And as hard as I press, I can barely feel the flower. Your touch is so—so—" What was the word? She stretched and issued a breezy contented sigh. "It's so amazingly soft that I—" She opened her eyes with a jolt.

His lips rested in a lazy part and his gaze had sharpened to ravenous intensity as he stared at her mouth. Smile faded, she sat up. Spell broken, his swift gaze found her eyes.

Yet not a speck of apology resided in them for him having looked at her like a beggar through a window at a feast. At first. Then an uncharacteristic contriteness came into his eyes. He lifted his face to the sky then. Sharp. Swift. He stared. Intense.

She looked up but saw nothing concerning or unusual. No funnel clouds or crashing planes or flaming parachutes or enemy missiles. Nothing spectacular that should so mightily hold a military rescuer's sudden avid interest. Or bind his eyes so intently to the sky.

Unless he felt bad for looking at her that way.

Not wanting him to feel condemned, she put her hand on his arm. "Vince?"

He shook his head. "Put it on." He gestured toward her wrist.

She held it up to eye the charms first. Her breath caught at the first one.

"A set of justice scales." Her vision rose from the bracelet, which dangled between them, to Vince, who she could see within the circle of the chain strand.

He averted his gaze. "Yeah, well, just so you know, that charm's my least favorite."

She laughed and lifted the second charm. "A tiny traffic light?"

"Yeah. Notice it's *red*. Which means *do not proceed*." He smirked. "A token of our friendship. How we met."

Her head fell back. "The wreck. Well, just so you know, this charm's *my* least favorite."

He snorted. "Why? Because you don't like to obey traffic signals?"

"No. Because I'm still ashamed of my actions." Her cheeks heated, but she laughed despite her embarrassment. This bracelet seemed a peace offering of sorts. Nothing short of a cleared hurdle.

If he could joke about it, he couldn't be all that mad still, right?

She lifted the third charm. "A tiny motorcycle?"

Now his cheeks tinged. "Yeah." He cleared his

throat. "So you don't forget about me once this all blows over."

"Blows over?"

"Yeah, this—this—" Hand on his bent knee, he flapped his fingers. "This mission you feel compelled to complete."

"A mission?"

"Yeah."

She faced him. "Is that what you think? That I see you merely as a mission and once my mission is met that I'll forget you?"

He shrugged. "Doesn't matter."

"I think it does." *To both of us.* "We're not just two ships passing in the night, Vince."

"No, we're two people crashing in an intersection."

She went to sock his arm. He leaned away, laughing. He caught her hand in his and didn't let go for a second.

Feeling too cozy, she slipped her hand from his. "Vince, I think we were meant to meet. Maybe not that dangerously intersected way, but still."

Uncomfortable with her words, she went back to studying his gift. "Pewter. My favorite."

"To match your empty-picture bracelet. Which you'll lose if you don't tighten."

"My aunt gave it to me. I haven't managed to purchase the gizmo to remove the links."

"I can do it for you. How is she, by the way?"

"My aunt? Set to come home next week. She's back to her spunky self."

And back to warning Val every day not to fall for the likes of Vince.

And every day she'd assured Aunt Elsie that she would never allow herself to fall for someone who didn't share her faith.

Now, looking at Vince, she knew her vow was going to be much more challenging than she'd thought.

In fact, the more time she spent with him, the more interested she became.

Which meant it was time to set a stronger guard on her heart.

He brushed a hand along her bracelet. "Why don't you put pictures into the little frames?"

She felt her skin grow hot, both her face and the area his fingers brushed. "Um, because Elsie said to save them for each of the children I've always wanted."

"Four kids?" His eyebrows rose.

"Four kids."

"Why four?"

"Because in an odd number, one will always feel left out."

"Four kids. Wow. Well, I think you'd be a great mom, Val." His words held sincerity as he held her gaze.

And for the first time in her life, Val envisioned the man she'd love to be married to when those children came forth.

And he was staring her right in the face and heart.

Jerking upright, she eyed her watch. "I've work to do. I should probably go." She stood.

A shadow passed over his face, clueing her that she'd been rude and ungrateful in her abruptness.

"Thanks for lunch." She patted her stomach. "The food was so good, and I ate so much, I hope I don't flatten the motorcycle tires."

He laughed and eyed her middle. "You've nothing to worry about."

He stood and tugged the field blanket up and, after rolling it, stuck it back in his saddlebag.

They'd stopped at the Market on Mayberry Street to pick up sandwiches and fruit from its deli. Pigged out really, was what they'd done.

But after riding for two hours then hiking for another three, they'd both been hungry and thirsty.

She swigged her last drop of water and tossed the plastic bottle in the recycling container next to the refuse can across the way.

Vince gathered the rest of their trash plus trash other park-goers had left. They met at the bike.

Likely his ponderous silence meant he'd picked up on her abrupt rising from the picnic blanket. But no matter what, no matter how much she enjoyed his companionship, she could not let him believe there was a future with them.

Couldn't allow herself to believe it either. Not unless he committed his heart and his future to God.

Each deep in companionable thought, they got on the bike. Scared her how naturally her arms came around his trim waist this time, whereas it had been awkward before.

Don't get used to holding him.

Until he belongs to God, he can never be yours.

"We still on for Monday at the pool?" he asked once they pulled into her driveway and he cut the engine.

"Yes." She slipped off the bike.

"And Talons on Tuesday?"

Her head whipped around. "Not on your—"

The protest died on her lips when she saw the teasing glint to his hooded eyes and open grin.

The kind of potent grin that could sentence a girl's heart to hammering like a judge's gavel.

Conversely, the kind of grin that could make a girl conveniently forget how difficult life could be with a spouse of a different faith.

Or worse, no faith.

Space. She needed space from him. And this dangerous draw, both physical and emotional.

"I may take a rain check on the PJ barbecue. I just remembered I have things to do."

Like figure out how to guard her suddenly vulnerable heart against devoting itself to him.

His face hardened to unreadable. He clenched his jaw and averted his gaze. "I understand."

And the sad thing was, she believed he truly did. Even the unspoken.

He started to step away. Her hand snaked out to touch his forearm. "I still want to be your friend."

He paused. Stared at the ground. Then her hand. "I know." He met her gaze. "But what if that's not enough for me?"

Her hands flew up. "God help you, it has to be."

"There you go, praying out loud again."

She lifted her face, fearing she'd angered him. But though his words leaned toward abrasive, his eyes held gentle humor. "So be it."

Let it be true! Help me reach him.

But help me do it without compromise.

She stepped onto her crumbling landing, remembering Elsie's words about building a solid foundation.

He stepped toward her.

She held out a forbidding hand. He paused. Eyed it. "Goodbye, Vince."

"I hope not for good. That sounds so final."

She stayed silent. Unable to honestly answer.

What about reaching out to Logan?

Vince could do that on his own.

What about reaching out to Vince?

God could do that on His own.

Her relationship with God came first. And she needed to keep her heart intact. If she kept being tempted to fall for him, she'd have to sever ties.

She backed into her living room and closed the screen door, creating a barrier between them. Symbolic and literal. "I hope not, too."

"See you Monday at the pool?" He shoved his hands into his pockets.

She bit her lip.

"If I can manage—" *not to start down this slippery slope of losing my heart to you* "—I'll be there."

Vince eyed her like she did pieces of evidence. "And if you don't go, how will Logan and the kids get there?"

"There are people from the church who loaned me the van. They could handle it for a few weeks." *Until I can manage to put you out of my heart and mind.*

Chapter Twelve

Vince hoped she could manage.

Whatever struggles were haunting her, he hoped she could fight them off. Or go to God and have Him do it.

His heart had twisted at the turmoil residing in her eyes. She wasn't the pillar he'd first thought.

And the last thing he wanted to be was her tempter.

Don't let me lead her astray. What she has with You, it's special. Don't let me mess it up, being the colossal screwup that I am.

But a sense of sadness swept Vince over his self-deprecating words. Like for once, he doubted the level of evil inside him.

Then another feeling washed over him.

One he could only describe as grief. Like maybe God was sad over Vince's words. But why would that be?

Unless God actually thought there was hope for him.

Having just worked his muscles to the max at Joel's gym, he slogged up the B and B steps and tugged out keys to the unit he shared with Chance.

Before he could stick his key in the door, it opened.

"Hey, Garrison."

"Hey." Chance stepped aside and let him in.

"What's up?" Vince set his keys on the table.

"Not much. You go work out?"

"Yeah. Sorry I didn't call. I needed to work off steam." Vince eyed the stack of messages on the table.

Chance handed him the four papers. "This one's from Aaron. He asked if you were still offering to watch the boys while he and Sarah go on their honeymoon."

"Sure." He loved watching Petrowski's twins. "Bryce and Braden are cool." And made him want kids of his own.

Someday maybe. With the right girl. Problem was, none of the typical one-night types he dated were ones he'd want to take marriage vows with. Definitely no motherly types. Val flashed across his mind. "It wasn't a date."

Chance looked up.

Vince laughed at himself. "Can't believe I blurted that out loud."

Chance shrugged. "Second message was from Val. Something about not being able to make it Monday."

"Really? Bummer." Disappointment scraped through him.

Chance lifted the next messages. "This was from a girl you hooked up with. Said she's free tonight. Call her. And the last message was your dad."

"What's that old geezer want?"

"To wish you happy birthday."

"Drunkard. My birthday was six months ago."

"So consider him being early for next year."

"Yeah. Right." Vince's heart sank. Because today was his brother's birthday. Not Vince's. "The alcohol is gonna kill him. Messes with his mind."

"Sorry, bud. Wish there was something I could do."

"Well, I know you've been sneaking off to Joel's prayer meetings. So I hope you've been tossing a few up for Dad."

"A few?"

"You know…prayers." Vince snorted. "What'd you think I meant? Cold ones?"

Chance's ears turned red. "Hey, I'm still your party buddy though. So's Brock."

"Yeah? I'm betting he crosses over to the dark side before you do."

Chance laughed. "You know, there really is something to the Bible. I've been reading stories of stuff God did. Some pretty cool stuff."

"Like what?"

"Dude, like he made an actual donkey talk."

"No kidding? Was his name Chance?"

Chance bashed him over the head with a newspaper.

Laughing, Chance shook his head. "You're impossible, man."

"But all things are possible with God."

Chance's head whipped up. "What did you just say?"

"You heard me."

"No, seriously. Say it again."

"I said all things are possible with God."

Chance paled. "Hey, I just read that." He motioned toward the Book on the table. "In there."

"Yeah. I've read it before. A lot of it. God might have helped all those other people. But he never helped my brother."

"Hey, I didn't mean to offend, man."

He shrugged. "You didn't. I'm tired. I'm heading to bed." He glanced at the messages on the table. Particularly the ones from his dad and from Val. And it was a toss-up as to which was more disappointing.

She'd cancelled. And his dad had forgotten which of his sons' birthday was today. Worse, he'd called to wish a dead man happy birthday.

Vince's gaze was drawn toward the message from the girl.

Strange. He'd have found solace in the physical before.

Vince didn't want to call an easy girl for once. And even stranger, he had no idea why. Nor had he wanted to go out partying lately.

Something in his world was far from right.

Maybe if he got a good night's sleep, one that

didn't contain images of Miss Distraction, when he woke up tomorrow his world would be back on its proper axis.

"Hey, Chance. I'm crashing, dude. I don't want to be woken up for anything. No matter who calls."

"Don't fret, Logan. I know who to call." Val clutched the phone and punched Vince's number again. Fingers trembled. She eyed Logan's face. Her stomach lurched but she put on her court face and paced her floor. Please answer this time!

Someone picked up on the fifth ring.

"H'lo."

"Vince, thank God! Sorry to startle you awake but I need you."

He coughed out a laugh. "Darlin', I'll never complain about a beautiful woman waking me up murmuring desperately that she needs me. Especially not one who dissed me hours before."

She slipped into the kitchen for privacy and an ice pack. "Logan's here. He's hurt."

Shuffling. Sounds like yanking covers back. Keys jangling. "Be right there."

And she knew he would, too.

His voice had instantly wakened on the line. Gone were the languid undertones of sleepiness and flirtation. The serious resolve in his voice infused her with relief.

"Thank you."

"See you in a few." He clicked off.

She went to sit again with Logan. "Hey, buddy." She pressed the ice packs to his eye and lip.

"You call the cops?"

"I promised you I wouldn't—yet. I called Vince. You need to go to the hospital for stitches."

"Mom don't have insurance."

"I'll pay."

"No. You make me go to the cops or the hospital, I'll run." He sniffed and wiped swollen eyes.

"Logan, please don't talk like that. I can't stand the thought of you being lost out there somewhere."

"Out there's better than home. Why's Mom stay with a mean guy?" Logan's cry came from a deep place. His voice seemed small, like a child's, not a self-sufficient teen.

"Maybe if she knew of the abuse, she'd make him leave. Have you told her?"

"No. He threatened to hurt her if I did."

"Logan, the police can help you. At least let me call Stallings. I believe your mom loves you enough to want you safe."

He sniffed. "Fine. How'm I gonna tell her?"

"Vince is on his way. He'll help us figure this out and make sure your mom is safe."

Val phoned Vince's cell back. Sounded like he was on his bike. She relayed the information Logan had shared.

"I'll make sure Refuge PD knows. I already called a local paramedic who skydives at the DZ. Name's Cole. He may beat me there," Vince said, then hung up.

Logan locked his fingers together and draped them over his knees. "When'll Vince be here?"

"In a few minutes."

He nodded and rocked back and forth.

"Where's the boyfriend now?"

"In bed, half-drunk."

"That could work in our favor."

A single headlight beam bounced across the yard and shone through the window as Vince pulled his motorcycle up. The deep rumble of its engine, a sound that had come to bring her a sense of anticipation and comfort, powered down.

"I'm scared. What if Moron hurts Mom? He said if I told he would."

"Vince won't let that happen."

"How do you know?"

She eyed Vince through the window. His resolve. His strength. His strenuous build. He seemed like the ultimate protector. Plus there were seven more just like him on the PJ team. "I just know. Trust me on this, okay?"

"Okay. But if something happens to Mom or Maddie, I'll never forgive you."

"Don't say that."

"Then don't risk their lives if you're not sure."

What if something went wrong? Doubt crept in like a robber stealing her peace.

Before Vince could knock on the door, Val let him in.

A paramedic named Cole also arrived and, once

inside, came straight to Logan. Knelt in front of him. "Hey, buddy. Val said you're hurt. Mind if I take a look?"

Logan shrugged. Then slid a sideways glance at Val.

She stood. "I'll step out for your privacy."

Vince stepped back. "Me, too."

"No, stay," Logan said to Vince.

Face tender with compassion and body language impassioned with fierce intent to protect, Vince moved close to Logan. Val stepped away, never feeling so glad for another human being in her life.

And in Logan's life.

Thank You. If he's this effective when he's not yet a Christian, I can envision the impact he'd make if he offered his full devotion to You. What kind, wonderful things he'd do.

Chapter Thirteen

He'd skin the creep alive.

Slowly.

Vince clenched his jaw at the cigarette burns along Logan's arms. Anger rocketed with every revealed mark and bruise inflicted by Logan's mom's hack of a boyfriend.

"I didn't do nothing to deserve this."

Vince nodded. "I know, buddy."

Logan sniffed.

"It's not your fault, Logan. You know that. Right?" Cole pulled out bandages and treated Logan's injuries.

"I know."

Stallings arrived in an unmarked police cruiser. He came in and hunkered between Cole and Vince, who knelt in front of Logan. "What happened?"

"Herman, Mom's boyfriend, or, as I call him, her Moron, called her bad names behind her back. So I stood up to him. Soon as she left for work, he cracked me with a lamp." Logan relaxed when Stallings nodded in an understanding manner and rested a supportive hand on his shoulder.

Stallings straightened. "Herman. Tall Caucasian guy with a snake tat on his neck and scars over his left eye?"

"Yeah, Herman Jones, aka Moron. Know him?"

"Unfortunately. Guy's got a rap sheet longer than Val's coffee table."

"What's that mean?"

"That means if you report him, he may never leave prison again," Val said.

"For real?"

"Where did he hit you?" Stallings pulled out a digital camera and a pad and started writing stuff down.

"On my arm." Logan raised it so Stallings could snap photos for his report.

Vince placed a fatherly hand on Logan's shoulder. "Buddy, we need to tell your mom what's going on."

"Yeah." Cole felt along Logan's swollen, bruised forearm. "Especially since I think it's broken."

"Yeah, so's the lamp. I blocked it with my arm."

Cole splinted the arm with temporary measures. "We'll need your mom's consent to treat you. We can't let this go."

Though Vince was a paramedic as well, he didn't have kid-size equipment handy. Plus Cole was a friend and Vince wanted to leave himself available to help Stallings deal with Moron and any cronies who may have dropped by Logan's mom's home since Logan had sneaked to Val's.

Refuge only had one officer on duty at a time, plus the sheriff. And since Steele was getting out there in weight and up there in age, he didn't count. He'd been looking to retire but Refuge hadn't found a suitable replacement yet.

Stallings shifted to look Logan over. "Where else did he hit you?"

"My back and ribs. He usually never hits me in the face because then people will see." Logan dipped his head and Vince knew instinctively he was humiliated by all this. His heart went out to Logan.

Vince motioned with his chin to Logan's cigarette burns. Stallings, eyes flashing the same fury Vince felt toward Moron, nodded and mouthed, "I see."

"He ever hit your mom?" Cole clenched his jaw.

"No. She'd kick his butt right out on the street."

Vince squeezed his shoulder. "I know how hard this kind of questioning is, Logan. I've lived it."

"You did?"

Vince nodded. "Only with neglect issues rather than physical abuse."

Nodding, Logan moved closer to Vince.

"You're a smart kid, Logan," Stallings said. "So I think you know deep down this isn't something you can keep from your ma."

Vince nodded agreement. "I've talked at length with your mom when she dropped by the DZ on her way from work to ask how your swim lessons were going. She needs to know what's going on so she can keep you safe."

"And so she can be safe," Cole added. "Because it's only a matter of time until he starts hitting on her, too. And she's so petite, he could really hurt her."

"You know her?"

Cole blushed. "We went to school together. But she probably doesn't remember me."

"Why, were you stuck up?"

Cole laughed. "No, she was. I was shy."

Logan grinned, for which Vince was glad. Logan looked to Val, who reentered the room. "You think he's right? That she could be in worse danger if I don't tell?"

Val nodded. "Unfortunately, I do."

Stallings stood. "Statistically speaking, they're right."

Logan blinked rapidly and appeared terrified at the notion. "And then there's Maddie to worry about."

Val reached for his hand. "Would you like me to tell your mom, Logan? Would that make it easier?"

He thought a minute. Literally chewed his lip. "No, I think she'd be upset that I came to another woman besides her. That you knew before she did is really gonna bother her. She won't care as much that I told Vince. But that I told another lady, well, you know, she's my ma."

"I understand." As a credit to Val, she truly looked like she did.

Vince had never been so glad for an attorney in his

life. Well, not an attorney exactly. But for Val's devotion to reach out to these kids.

Had she not spent significant time and money and effort doing that, Logan might not have felt he could come to her, which meant he might not have been helped.

"And it doesn't hurt that she's the county prosecutor," Vince said.

Val's head snapped up.

Logan looked around. "Who? Val?"

Vince nodded. "She can see to it that the guy's put away."

"For real? Can you?"

Val recovered from her obvious shock at his positive statement and nodded. And for once Vince wanted her to know he saw the good side of the law.

And God only knew what would have gone on in that household had Logan not felt he had someone to turn to.

Yes, God only knew.

And He sent Val to intervene.

And used Vince, too?

The thought streaked through him like an F-22 crossing enemy sky. It felt so odd, so foreign yet spellbinding. The possibility that God might have a purpose for Vince's life. Before meeting Val, he'd have never believed God might have an honorable plan for him. But now…

Taking a chance on the prompting he felt bubble, Vince faced Logan. "Want me to talk to your mom?"

"I was thinking that, but I was afraid to ask." Logan ran his hands down the new jeans Vince bought him last week. He'd surprised Logan by dropping by unannounced. Picked him up for the bike ride Logan had begged for. Afterward, Vince took him clothes shopping.

"Be more than happy to," Vince added.

Logan stood. "Okay. Yeah, let's tell her. But let me break it to her first. You give her the gory details." He eyed his swollen arm.

Val paced while Logan phoned his mother at work. The way Val's lips moved and her manner of calm focus reminded Vince of the intersection, when she'd prayed for him.

Vince hoped Logan felt the sense of peace Vince had when, even in the face of his barbed protests, Val had prayed.

After Logan spoke to his mom, he handed the phone to Vince, who stepped into Val's kitchen and explained about Logan's arm and their plan. She confessed that she'd been stashing money aside to be able to get herself and the kids safely away and would willingly press charges.

Vince returned. "She's coming home from work."

Logan stood. "We need the money. I feel bad she's taking off for me."

"Bud, I know you feel crummy about it. But as upset as your mom was on the phone, there's no doubt in my mind she loves you."

"I wish she'd find a good guy like you. But I'm glad you have Val."

Bad as Vince wanted to correct Logan's misconception about him and Val, now was not the time. He needed to focus on Logan and righting his jacked-up home situation.

"What else did Mom say?"

"For you to stay here while she talks to Moron."

Terror crossed Logan's face. "I'm scared of what he'll do."

"Stallings and I will stand in the yard. Not close enough for him to see us but close enough to intervene if things go south. Soon as he leaves, Stallings will pull him over for a routine stop, then nail him on warrants."

"Like, arrest him?" Logan asked.

"On the spot," Stallings said.

Logan nodded. "Thanks. That makes me feel better." His eyes squished. "Wait, what'll you pull him over for?"

"Busted taillight," Vince said and eyed his watch. "I'll head down in twenty. She'll be home in thirty. Think Moron'll still be there?"

"Yeah. All he does is party all night, sleep all day."

"How's he get money?" Stallings asked.

Logan cocked his head. "You didn't hear this from me, but, I think he's a dealer. And I'm not talking cards."

Stallings nodded. "I suspected. Does he often have strangers over?"

"Yeah," Logan confirmed. "Every few hours."

"Which means they could be there now." Stallings faced Vince. "If this guy's been running the drug ring we've been investigating, we may need more help."

"Want me to call a few buddies for backup?" Vince was acutely aware that teammate Manny's wife Celia's first husband was killed during a DEA sting near this part of town years ago.

He didn't want Refuge to lose another officer. Stallings had become his friend. Much as he loved Sheriff Steele, the guy couldn't outrun to apprehend a turtle if his life depended on it.

"Can't hurt. Since you guys are military police of sorts and this sits so close to the base."

"You're military police?" Logan's eyes lit. "I love the service. Can't wait to join."

"He's not only military. He's an elite special operative," Val shared, sparks of pride in her gorgeous gray eyes. "But legally, Stallings will do the actual arresting."

Once Vince tore his gaze away and figured out how to operate his cell again, he phoned his team.

"Whoa, dude. Are you really Special Forces?" Logan asked once Vince ended the call.

"Air Force Special Ops, yes."

"I just thought you were a killer swim instructor. What is it you do?"

"Mainly rescue pilots and other military personnel shot down or crashed behind enemy lines. We're combat skydiving paramedics. We also perform civilian rescues."

Logan scrambled closer. "Like what?"

"Recently, help hurricane and Midwest flood victims. Pluck stranded climbers off Everest and Mount Hood. Rescued a youth group lost in Yellowstone. Stood by for space-shuttle launches. Minor stuff like that."

"*Minor* stuff? Dude, how can I be what you are?"

"I'm a pararescue jumper. PJ for short. Look it up online. If you're still sure that's what you want to be when you grow up, once you graduate high school, I'll take you to a recruiter, with your mom's permission."

"Dude, Mom would love it. She says the military would give me discipline and help me pay for college and stuff."

Stallings faced Logan again. "I'll patrol your home closely for the next few months, too."

Logan nodded. "Thanks."

Cole knelt and dabbed salve on Logan's burns. "Logan, I wish you'd press charges so we can put this guy away so he can't hurt anyone else."

Logan looked to Vince. "Think I should?"

"Yes. I also think Cole's right that you should let one of us take you to the hospital for treatment."

"I will. But after stuff goes down with Mom and Moron."

Moments later a truck full of people showed up.

Logan's eyes bugged. "Wow. All these guys came to help Mom and me?"

"Of course, bud."

"Thanks for going to all this trouble for me. For us." His eyes darted between Val and Vince. He sniffled.

Vince scrubbed knuckles over Logan's head and pulled him in for a sideways man-hug, avoiding his injured arm. "We care about you, Logan. You mean a lot to us. And we certainly don't consider you, or any of the other teens, trouble. Okay?"

Logan nodded and swiped fingers across his eyes.

Val blinked back tears. "Excuse me. I'll let the posse in." She grabbed Vince's hand on the way to the door and squeezed. "Thank you," she whispered.

Vince swallowed hard and squeezed back. Val proceeded to the door. This situation with Logan had yanked at both their heartstrings. Not only that, it seemed to have tied their heartstrings in a knot with each other.

His team entered.

Joel approached Vince. "We're ready. Stallings is using our team for backup because we're used to combat."

Logan grabbed Vince's shirtsleeve. "Wait, wait. I'm really scared. What if you mess up?"

"We won't. Stallings has SWAT training and we're stealthy. Per your mom's request, Aaron's fiancée, Sarah, picked up Maddie from your grandma's where she stays at night or when day care's closed. She's safe. And we'll have your mother safely out of the house before Moron can blink."

"Dude, but Moron has a sawed-off shotgun. I took

all the shells I could find and hid them, but he might have more somewhere. Why don't you pray? It'd be better if you had God helping you," Logan sputtered. "If you really care about me like you say, then do it. Before you go in there, please pray."

The battle grew evident on Vince's face. Everyone strained to see what he'd say. How he'd react.

Compassion glistened in Vince's eyes. He knelt. "Logan, I'll be straight with you. I'm not a praying man. I don't honestly know if He'd even hear me. But if it'd make you feel better, I'll pray."

"And mean it?"

Vince nodded. "And mean it."

The room crackled with surprise and intense emotion.

Val met Joel's gaze. Tears glistened. She'd learned from Sarah that Joel had been praying for Vince's salvation for half a decade.

Stallings, also looking wondrously sobered with awe, peered out the curtain. "Logan's mom's car is coming down the end of the road. It's about time to go."

Vince pulled Logan close. "So, uh, God, help Logan. I'm sure You know what's going on. Be with us as we take care of business."

"Help Mom to lose the jerk. Thanks for Stallings and Cole and the PJs and most of all for Val and Vince. And, help Mom be like Val and find a decent guy, too."

Val's eyes popped open. Vince looked momentarily startled, too.

They needed to help Logan understand they were only friends.

Now to convince her bleating heart's little blips of hope it was so.

Thirty minutes later had Moron cuffed and cursing in the back of Stallings' cruiser.

Logan's mom hugged Val. "Thank you for befriending me and Logan. Now that Hermon is out of our lives for good, we'll be safe." She rubbed a hand along Logan's bangs. "And next time, I'll make better choices in a guy." Tears bubbled then streamed from her eyes as she gently hugged her son. "I love you, Logan."

"Love you, too, Mom." Logan grinned and hugged his mom back with his good arm, then eyed Vince. "I'm sure he has single friends in Refuge who are decent guys, Mom." Logan's gaze traveled to Stallings and Cole. "Chin up."

Val clasped Vince's hand and squeezed. He squeezed back, communicating that he, too, was touched by Logan and thankful for the resolution as well as convinced of his mom's love and devotion to keeping her children safe and making their home a better place, even at great personal cost to herself. Of course, when she learned of the rap sheet on her loser ex, she'd probably be even happier to be rid of him.

Vince released her hand, which reminded her they were still holding hands. Her cheeks warmed.

For once, Val didn't want to let him go. But just as Moron wasn't a good fit for Logan's mom, she and Vince didn't have a future unless major, heart-felt and life-altering decisions took place.

"We're just friends," Val said while combing Elsie's hair after her bath Thursday night. Val had carried a sense of thankfulness all day that Moron had confessed without a hitch.

She hoped Vince would take that as God having answered his prayers for Logan and the situation.

"So you say. You've been talking about him like he's syrup on your pancakes. Mark my words—you're getting sweet on him."

"No, Elsie. I promise I'm not."

"Well, if you aren't, you will be soon enough. Especially if he's everything you say he is."

"What's that supposed to mean?" Val set down the brush and picked up Elsie's slippers.

"All you used to do was complain about him. Now, you can't say enough good about him."

"Evidence God is working in his heart."

"Best be sure He's working in yours, too. Because like it or not, you're a-fallin' for this guy. No one looks forward this much to spending four days in a row with someone who's just a *friend*."

Useless to argue. But arguing was what Val got paid for in court. Besides, not like this was a vain argument anyway.

"You're imagining things. Must have bumped your noggin when that scooter did gymnastics down those stairs." She helped Elsie tug her sock on.

Elsie chuckled, then braced her hands along Val's cheeks. "Honey, let's be serious here. If anyone needs a good bump on the noggin, it's you for fooling yourself."

Val straightened. "How am I fooling myself?"

"To think you can spend that much time with a man you are *so* attracted to and interested in...and not have your heart end up involved. It's naïveté in the third degree."

Wordlessly, Val assisted Elsie from the bathroom to her bed.

"Speaking of the third degree, I feel bad you having to stay here with me when you have a big case coming up."

"Oh, please. I love spending time with you. I consider it an honor to help you. You took care of me when I broke my elbow, remember?"

"I do." Elsie's deep-set eyes sparkled.

"Besides, I concentrate better here. And you're right. It's a big case. Not a lot of hard evidence."

"That's tough."

"Yeah."

Val had been working mostly from home to keep an eye on Elsie. Her mom, who lived an hour away, took turns sitting with Elsie during the days Val had court. Nurses had come in to teach Val to assist Elsie with care and activities of daily living.

"Cases like this especially bother me since meeting Vince."

"Why, is he a convict?"

Val laughed. "No. His brother was wrongly convicted. A fraudulent witness later admitted perjury. Vince's brother died in prison before he could be formally cleared of charges."

"But he was cleared?"

"Unofficially."

"Maybe you can work your legal wonders and make it official."

"That crossed my thoughts also, Elsie. Great minds think alike, huh?"

Elsie's smile brightened then faded. "Sweetie, on some things, I don't want you a-thinkin' like me or following in my footsteps. Especially not fooling myself and falling for an unbeliever. Promise you won't marry him."

"Vince isn't the marrying type."

"Uh-huh. Someday he's going to change his mind. Speaking of minds, don't be surprised if I give him a piece of mine when we meet tomorrow."

Val laughed. "I have a feeling he's tough enough to take it."

"Remember all I endured. Be wiser with your choices. If that man does not follow God, do not fall for him."

Chapter Fourteen

"It's free fall or not at all." Vince leaped from the plane for Friday parachute training. His team streamed out behind him.

They'd been practicing HALO jumps before daybreak. With the end of their workday dawning, they were just jumping for fun.

Speaking of fun, he'd see Val in a matter of hours.

Exhilaration blew through him—partly free-fall rush, partly anticipation of seeing Val.

Soon as he ran home and got a shower, he'd head to her house. Help her prepare for the youth bash and meet Aunt Elsie. Saturday, he'd head back to her place, pick her up and bring her to the PJ barbecue.

Then, after church Sunday, she'd promised to go for a motorcycle ride if weather permitted.

Church. Sunday.

He was actually going to step foot inside a church.

On purpose.

Without being dead, buried or married.

Unbelievable.

Wow. A whole weekend of Val-related activities. Even if he had to suffer through a church service, time with her would be worth it.

He pulled the rip cord on his parachute and toggled until his boots glided to a dry spot of earth.

Refuge needed the rain this week would bring. And he needed the refreshment Val provided for his parched soul.

He was also looking forward to meeting Val's aunt.

After showering, Vince wore holes in the floor of the B and B unit he and Chance rented.

"Why're you so antsy?" Chance stuck sunglasses on his head and watched Vince pace.

"Clock's not moving."

Chance laughed. "Hot date tonight or something?"

"I'm seeing Val. But I wouldn't call it hot."

"Why not? She's a total babe."

"Yeah, but we're not an item. I'm going over there to help her with the neighborhood kids' youth bash."

"Sounds fun."

"Wanna come?"

"Another time. I'm headed out of town to see my folks. I'll be back for the PJ cookout tomorrow."

"Have fun."

"Later."

Vince eyed the clock. Time crawled. Still three hours before he was scheduled to be at Val's. She lived less than twenty minutes away. Maybe he'd go back to the DZ. See if Joel needed anything. Helmet on, he hopped on his bike and headed out.

After arriving, he went into the office. Petrowski sat talking to Joel.

Vince knocked on the open door. "Am I interrupting?"

Petrowski waved him in. "Nah. Have a seat."

Vince straddled a chair. "Got anything for me to do? I've a couple hours to kill."

"Can't think of anything. You?" Petrowski asked Joel.

"Not unless you want to rig chutes." Joel grinned.

Vince laughed. "No, thanks. I'd rather chew steel nails."

"Word on the street is you eat them for breakfast." Petrowski knuckled Vince's forehead. "Although you've been in better moods the past months."

Brock entered, sipping a soda. He paused in front of Vince. "Thought you left."

"I did. I'm back killing time."

"Beats killing something else, I guess." Sitting, Brock leaned his chair back on two legs to look at Vince. "It's Friday. We hitting pubs tonight?"

Vince scraped a hand along his neck, which suddenly heated like the exhaust of his bike on full throttle. "Uh, I kinda already have plans."

Brock sighed. "I see how it is. I'm chopped liver these days."

"Hey, no one said you can't go clubbing alone."

Brock socked Vince's arm. "You're the life of the party, man. Least you used to be. It's not the same without you. Since when did you sprout a conscience anyway?"

"You guys coming to the cookout this weekend?" Joel asked, probably to distract Brock from picking on Vince and Vince from retaliating by punching Brock's front teeth out.

"It's at my house this time," Petrowski added.

Brock rocked his chair back farther. "You kidding, man? Wouldn't miss it."

Vince put his foot on the rail of Brock's chair to keep him from falling back and busting his head. He eyed Joel. "Meeting those little kids you've waited on for so long? I'm there, dude."

"Yeah. They're awesome. Well-behaved. Polite. Funny." Joel's eyes sparkled with many things Vince had longed to see in the eyes of his own dad.

"Amber and I are having them dedicated this weekend at church. It's gonna be pretty cool," Joel added.

Vince cleared his throat. "Speaking of church, what time does yours start?"

Total.

Dead.

Silence.

Vince's ears heated as the three men stared, literally open-mouthed.

Petrowski was first to clamp his mouth shut. He leaned in. "Did you just ask what time *church* started?"

Vince grew irritated. "Yeah. But not for me. That attorney I've been seeing, well, as a friend anyway, she's looking for a good church." Vince moved his foot from Brock's seat.

A big, creaky clank sounded as Brock's chair legs flew back, back, back. Vince, Joel and Petrowski reached.

Too late.

Brock flailed his arms with a helpless expression. *Slam!*

"Dude! You all right?" Vince gripped Brock's forearm and helped him up.

Brock rubbed his head. "Not the smartest thing I've ever done." He reoccupied the chair Petrowski righted while Joel tried his best to cover snickers with his hand.

Brock groaned. "Vince's fault."

"Me? I didn't push you back, man. You leaned."

Brock stood, then sat, then stood and turned in wacky circles. "Dude, I'm like freaking here. One second you ask what time church starts. Next you mention attorney and seeing and friend in the same sentence. You haven't gone clubbing since February. And clerks at the liquor store ask if you died because you haven't been in." Brock finally sat. "Dude, that wreck did something to you."

"Maybe a world of good." Joel leaned forward.

Vince shot Joel and Brock a toxic look. "Musta hit my head and acquired temporary brain damage."

Brock started to lean his chair back again but must

have thought better of it, because he leaned forward until all four legs rested on the floor. "Hope it doesn't happen to me." He rubbed the back of his head.

Vince faced Joel and Petrowski. "So anyway, about church. I know you guys wouldn't be going there if it was a cult or something. She's new to town and with her aunt's recent accident, she hasn't had a chance to find a church she likes yet."

"I'll have Sarah offer to pick her up Sunday if she wants."

"Uh, well, actually, I was thinking of picking her up."

"And taking her to church?" Joel craned his neck.

"Yeah, but don't get your hopes up, Montgomery. I'm only doing it to stick by my word."

Brock's hands waved beside his head in frantic winglike maneuvers. "Dude, explain to me *how* you managed to give your word about going to church? I'm in the Twilight Zone here."

"We had an air-hockey challenge. The winner got to take the loser anywhere they choose. She chose church."

"So you lost the game?" Brock laughed.

Vince scowled. "No. We tied."

"So where'd you take her? Or should I bother asking?" Brock folded arms across his chest.

"I didn't take her to bed if that's what you're insinuating. It's not like that with us. She's a nice girl."

"I can't believe I'm hearing this. You've been seeing a girl and *nothing's* happened?" Brockton clicked his tongue.

"Nope. Nothing. And I told you, we're not really seeing each other that way. We're friends. But even if we were seeing each other as more than friends, nothing would still happen. And for once, it's refreshing."

"Refreshing? Dude. You are sounding more and more like a female deodorant commercial every time your mouth opens." Brock put dismayed hands on his head. "This does not sound like you at all, Reardon. What changed?"

"Maybe I've changed. What I want out of life. I'm rethinking a lot of stuff."

Again a conscious stream of quiet followed Vince's words, proving he'd shocked them all into silence.

Joel stood, very still and quiet. No secret to anyone how long Joel, and later Petrowski, had been praying for the team to come into a relationship with Jesus.

Joel unfolded his arms. "I'm glad you met her, Reardon. She's been good for you."

"Then why do I get the vibe you're concerned?"

"Frankly, I'm cautious of your motives." Joel hawkeyed Vince.

"Hey, I admit I love a good challenge. But she's not some conquest. I'd never disrespect her like that."

"You won't try to compromise her faith?" Petrowski asked.

"No, Aaron. Not on purpose. Our relationship isn't physical."

Another layer of silence fell. They knew the potential existed for unintended emotional involvement.

But they had nothing to worry about.

"And as far as us falling in love, that's never gonna happen. In the remote event one of us did, we'd never act on it. She knows what she wants in a forever kinda guy. And I *definitely* do not fit the description."

Chapter Fifteen

"He fits the description." Elsie peeked out the curtain beside her transfer chair. "Tall, dark and covered in leather as black and sleek as his buzzed hair and brooding eyes."

Sure Elsie wasn't watching, Val sneaked a fresh coat of lipstick on. And finger-styled her hair. And dabbed a dot of concealer on the blemish on her chin.

She shouldn't look so forward to seeing him. Especially not since he'd meet Elsie tonight. And if she knew Elsie, she'd give Vince the third degree as soon as he walked in the door.

Then again, that might be a good thing.

A reminder to them both to keep this firmly rooted in the realm of friendship. Since Elsie was still not looking, Val yanked out her mascara wand and applied another coat.

"Quit primpin'. He'll have a hard enough time

keeping his hands off of you as it is," Elsie said, still staring out the window.

Val whirled. "Elsie!" The woman still had eyes in the back of her head.

The doorbell rang. Val smoothed hands down her pants and stepped toward the door.

Whirring into motion, Elsie wheeled herself to it first. "I want to have a firm word with this young man. Make sure he acts appropriately with you this evening."

Val tried to step over the chair to reach the door first. "Elsie, we're *just* friends. In no way is this a date." Val opened the door.

And there stood Vince with an enormous heart-shaped box of candy and a lavish bouquet of long-stemmed red roses in crisp green-and-white parchment paper.

And, oh my, he had on a tie! A silky black number riddled with a conglomeration of skulls, but still. A tie, nonetheless. And a button-up shirt with sharp silver studs for buttons. She'd never seen him so dressed up.

"Hey, babe." He grinned.

Babe? Val's face flamed. She glared at the roses. The candy. The formal-for-Vince attire. Then at him.

Even his heavy-duty Harley boots looked like he'd given them a shine.

And, was that manly cologne? She leaned in. Sniffed.

His wide grin morphed into a smirk.

Like he'd done this on purpose.

Hands on her hips, Val narrowed her gaze.

"You gonna let him in, or stand there gawking and snorting at him all night?" Elsie shooed Val and tugged on her shirt.

Val stepped aside to let the vagrant enter.

With the flowers.

And the candy in the velvety heart-shaped box.

Why on earth had he brought romantic things and dressed in a way that made this look like a date?

Well, she supposed she should give him the benefit of the doubt and be as polite as her ire would let her.

Val reached for the flowers. "Thanks. I'll just take these and put them in wat—"

He moved the flowers from her reach. "They're not for you, Val. Don't look so flustered."

Val's mouth opened but no words came to mind.

Stepping in, Vince chuckled and pressed the door closed with his motorcycle boot. He bent and kissed Elsie on her cheek. Then he displayed a lavish courtly bow and presented the flowers to her. "They're for Elsie."

"I'm a diabetic," Elsie said, eyes grown wide.

Vince nodded and presented the candy. "Not to worry, milady. These are sugar-free. And approved by the American Diabetic Association."

Elsie's hands snapped up to cover her cheeks. He pinkening cheeks. Val rolled her eyes.

"Well, if this doesn't beat all I ever seen." Elsie took the flowers and batted gracious eyes at Vince

"Thank you. I can't remember the last time I got flowers from a fellow as handsome as you." She settled the candy in her lap. "Why, I'm—I'm—"

"Like all women when it comes to Vince. Completely smitten," Val muttered and shoved her feet into her shoes.

She sighed long and made a notable display of eyeing her watch, hoping to get out of there before the feathers hit the fan if Elsie decided to come out of her twitterpated haze and tear into Vince—who wasn't seeming to get Val's hints that she wanted to leave. Well, subtlety wasn't her greatest gift. "Ready to go, Vince?"

"Actually, we have a little time." Unhurried, he peeled off his jacket and hung it in her closet.

Her closet!

Since when did he come in here and make himself at home?

Val eyed Elsie, who hawkeyed Val. And she realized his actions must seem as though he was familiar with her home. Which he most certainly was not.

Val cleared her throat. "Actually, I wouldn't mind getting to town and back a little early."

"Actually, I'd like to stay and visit Elsie awhile. We have plenty of time to run to the market before the kids get here," Vince said calmly.

Val resisted the urge to make grumbling noises. Her eyes veered toward the candy. How she loved chocolate. She released a winsome sigh. And those flowers were gorgeous!

Pings of envy went through her. But also a softening worked its way in over Vince's thoughtfulness toward Elsie. Just when she thought she had Vince pegged, another layer peeled back and she saw deeper. The view always surprised and, unfortunately, pleased her.

Vince stepped toward the bird cage as though mesmerized by the brilliant green-and-yellow cockatiel. "What's its name?"

"Pretty Boy. I wouldn't get too close. He can be cantankerous," Val warned.

Elsie watched them both carefully.

Vince leaned close to the cage. Val expected feathers to fly and the bird to put up a fluttery chirpy ruckus.

But he made birdie-purr noises and leaned his torso to the left and to the right in a primping, preening dance.

"Can I hold him?" Vince asked Elsie.

"Well, he normally bites people he doesn't know."

Val held up bandaged fingers. "And sometimes people he does know. He can be as unpredictable as you, Vince."

He put his hands on the door of the cage and smiled at Elsie. "May I?"

"At your own risk." Elsie waved him on.

Vince opened the cage door, reached in his hand and held his finger in front of the branch perch.

The bird hopped onto his finger. Vince withdrew his hand from the cage with Pretty Boy attached.

"Hi, Pretty Boy." Vince brought the bird close to his face. Eye to eye. "According to Val, I'm Bad Boy."

"Be careful, young man," Elsie warned.

Val stepped close with the feather duster, should she need to rescue Vince in the event of a domestic bird attack. "Vince, he bites."

"So do I." Vince made chirping noises at the bird.

"Hi, Pretty Boy. Hi, Pretty Boy. Hi, Pretty Boy. *Yuwaaaack,*" came from the bird's throat. He hopped off Vince's finger onto his shoulder and hopped around in playful, wacky circles. "Pretty Bad Boy, Pretty Bad Boy, Pre-eh-ety."

"Well, isn't that something." Elsie shook her head and used her good leg to move herself closer. "The last person able to tame that bird like that was my late husband."

Elsie's words halted Val's amazement at Vince's handling of the bird and Pretty Boy's calm reaction.

"Yeah, Vince reminds me of Uncle Parcel in more ways than one."

And Val was glad for the reminder since Pretty Boy wasn't the only one falling under Vince's magnetic charm. "In fact, Elsie, remember how Uncle would use the bird as an excuse not to go to church with you? He'd stay home every Sunday just to sit with the bird."

Spell broken, Elsie's eyes sharpened and her gaze narrowed. "I do remember that. Parcel would spend every Sunday sitting with the bird instead of sitting in the pews with me. While I went to church for years."

"Alone." Immovable knot in her throat, Val slipped into the other room. She rubbed warmth back into her arms.

Vince, bird still on his shoulder, followed her to the fridge. "Hey, beautiful," he said, low and close.

She whirled. "You *are* a charmer. Smooth move with the flowers, Casanova." She yanked her youth bash shopping list off the fridge.

Pretty Boy squawked and flew at her.

"Whoa!" She ducked before he could tangle his claws in her hair. He made another pass, swooping razor-close to her head, then zoomed up onto the curtain rod, his favorite place to sit.

Val removed her hand from her throat. "That bird loves terrorizing me. Dive-bombs my head every time I turn around."

"He is adorably disgruntled." Vince laughed. "But then again, so are you."

"Why do you say that?"

"It offended you when I pulled the flowers from your reach."

"Did not!" She tossed a dish towel in the sink.

"I'd never offend you on purpose, Val."

"You've offended half the planet already, bad boy. Why stop now?" The last part spilled out in a giggle. She squared her feet to face off with him.

Matching her stance, he crossed loose arms over his chest in a Mr. Clean stance. "You were jealous because I brought Elsie candy and flowers and not you." He lifted his chin, challenging her to deny it.

Never one to pass up a challenge, she lifted her chin higher. "I was not. I could care less." Wistfulness washed over her. "Were there any caramels in those chocolates?"

He released an openmouthed laugh. "Yes, but they're sugar-free and taste terrible."

"Terrible?"

"Yes. Terrible. Insanely awful. Like mildewed cardboard. Trust me. You wouldn't like them." He held out his hand above hers. "But it just so happens I did bring you something. Thought I'd present it in private so Elsie doesn't get any weird ideas."

Val held her hand below his.

"For the collection accruing on your bracelet." He dropped three tiny new charms in her palm.

"Oh! A little blue briefcase, a pair of pink flip-flops and a sterling silver life jacket!"

"Yeah, for when you fell in the pool."

She laughed.

"Come on, grace. Let's get stuff ready for the youth bash." Vince reached up to the curtain rod, and Pretty Boy hopped onto his finger and rode there on the "perch."

Voices drifted into earshot as they reentered the living room. Vince slid Pretty Boy, singing, back into the cage.

Val's mom, talking to Elsie, turned to smile at Val. "Let myself in. Hope you don't mind."

Val hugged her mom. "Of course not." She turned to Vince. "Mom, this is Vince Reardon. The para-rescue jumper I told you about. Vince, this is my mom, Toni."

"Ma'am." Vince stepped forward to shake Val's mom's hand.

"So you're the one whose bike she crashed. I assure you, sir, I taught my daughter to drive better than that."

Vince laughed. "I hope so."

"But I hear she's using her van money to replace your bi—"

"Mom!" Val smooshed her hand up against her mother's mouth. What if her mom had spilled that Val had been trying to contact Vince's sister about rebuilding the bike? Hadn't Val told her mom the bike rebuilding was confidential?

Val slid a sidelong look at him.

Vince's smile had at some point faded. His dark-ening eyes monitored Val and Toni as closely as a forensics expert might study a murder suspect's DNA signature under magnification.

And for the first time in a long time, his dark, brooding mask fell back into place.

Chapter Sixteen

His day just jumped on a rocket and shot south. Bad as he wanted to haul out of there, hop on his bike and tear up the highway, he promised Logan he'd be at this bash.

For Logan, he wouldn't go back on his word.

What was Val up to? He watched her pick up Elsie's suitcase and shoo her mom out the door.

"Trouble in paradise?" Elsie asked while Vince wheeled her down the ramp.

"There is no paradise."

"There could be."

"Meaning?" Crazy lady.

"She has a good heart. And it seems you do, too. Or Pretty Boy wouldn't have taken to you."

Okay, maybe not so crazy. Wise would be more like it. "Thanks, Elsie. Your opinion means a lot."

"But it's not the one that matters most. Is it?"

Vince paused to study her, not sure what she was

getting at nor desiring to know. "If you say so, Elsie." Vince lifted her from the chair and rested her in the passenger seat of Toni's town car. "Have a good weekend."

"You, too."

Val waved as the women pulled away. Vince thrust his hands in his pockets. "Gonna tell me what she—"

"No." Val rubbed her arms and turned toward her car. "At least not yet."

He reached out his hand.

She stared at it.

"The list?" he said impatiently.

Pain flashing across her eyes at his tone nearly broke the hardening he felt happening inside.

She slipped him the list. "Oh, right. I planned to go with you—"

He shook his head.

She stepped back, nodded.

He hopped on his bike and revved the gas, needing to release the power and the pressure building inside. He pulled from her driveway with a horrible feeling attaching itself to him.

For the first time in a long time he didn't feel like a team with Val. And he didn't like this disconnected feeling. Nor the pain in her eyes reflected in his handlebar mirror.

But no matter. She'd brought this on herself. This distrust. She was keeping something from him. Which made him question her motives. If she was only reaching out to him for pity or trying to right some wrong, he wanted nothing to do with her or whatever little personal code-of-justice game she was secretly playing to appease her case of personal guilt.

Once back, Vince felt calm enough to carry on a semi-normal conversation. Except for the heavy weight of concern in her apprehensive eyes as they returned time and time again to rest on him when she thought he wasn't looking.

He set bags on her counter. "Let's get things ready."

"Yeah, the kids will start popping in here any minute." She moved close but not as close as usual. Her motions were more tentative.

"What's for dinner? Kids always want to eat."

"I'm bubbling hot dogs." She headed to the kitchen.

"Bubbling?" Concerned, he followed her to the freezer. She pulled out packages of frozen franks. "Got any already thawed?"

"I didn't think to do that. I'm not exactly a whiz in the cooking department." She stuck them in the microwave and hit six minutes.

"Whoa!" Vince pushed the off button. "Val, you can't cook those for six minutes. They'll explode or catch fire."

She giggled. "Why do you think I said I was bubbling them?"

The doorbell rang. Several teens ventured in. Val

opened the microwave and reached for a package of hot dog buns.

Turning away, Vince handed the teens a stack of paper plates. "You guys set these out on the picnic table."

More teens arrived. Two carrying basketballs. "Care if we play?" they asked Val.

"Go right ahead." She gestured toward the backyard and poured ice into a large plastic tub.

Vince held open the door for them then turned back around to an acrid smell hitting him in the face. He looked around for the source.

"Fire!" Logan pointed to the microwave.

Vince leaned forward, peering at the glowing ball. "Wow. Yeah. Definite flameage going on in there." He jerked the cord out of the wall. "Val, what'd you put in there?"

"Just a package of hot dog buns." Her eyes widened.

Vince wrapped a moist towel around his hand. "Stand back," he ordered as he pushed open the microwave door. Smoke billowed out.

"Wow!" Logan scrambled back, eyes wide.

"Loganflliponthewater," Vince said as one word, and then he covered the fist-sized fire with the wet towel and ran it to the sink. Smoke sizzled beneath the water.

Vince dropped the glob in the sink and aimed the faucet sprayer toward the heap. The detector started screeching above their heads. Pretty Boy mimicked the beep sound from the other room.

Fire out, Vince faced Val. He lifted the shriveled plastic sack which held the charred buns. "This caused it." He pointed to a metal bread tie, now black, with melted plastic partially covering it.

"Oh. I didn't know the tie was still on there." Cheeks reddening, Val turned away. Wanting to distract from her embarrassment, Vince said to Logan, "Hey did you know that bread has different colored ties for each day of the week? White. Green. Yellow. Red. Blue. And I think orange. That's how you know whether the bread is fresh that day or not."

"Cool," Logan said and headed outside.

Vince came behind Val, hands on her shoulders. Standing behind her, he had the strongest urge to lean and plant a kiss on her head. Took enormous effort to exercise restraint. "Hey, no need to be embarrassed."

She laughed. "Thanks. I tried to warn you that I'm a disaster in the kitchen." Her eyes sparkled.

"Then you are officially not allowed to be alone in the same room with that oven unless accompanied by a responsible adult. You scare me." Vince chuckled and tried hard to disengage his gaze from Val's.

Humor evidenced in her face yet the connection lasted.

Vince reluctantly tore his gaze away and checked on the teens. "How about we finish cooking these hot dogs on your grill."

"My what?"

"Grill. Big metal thing that sits outside on four legs and barbecues or smokes meat and stuff?"

Her cheeks tinged. "I know what a grill is."

"Do you use charcoal or gas?"

"If I had one, I'd use charcoal. Because if I owned a gas grill, I'd probably blow up the neighborhood. Boom. Right off the map."

He laughed. "I don't doubt it. No biggie. I'll call Brock. Have him bring my grill."

She sighed. "I am so inept in the kitchen."

"But I'll bet you're killer in the courtroom." He winked, feeling release from tension for the first time since Toni's words had tossed a verbal grenade at him.

"Is that meant to be sarcastic?"

"I'm not entirely sure," Vince answered honestly.

"Fair enough. So you call Brock and I'll go see what the kids are up to in the backyard. I put a basketball hoop up, so I imagine they're shooting hoops."

"*You* put it up?"

"Yeah. I used to play. That's how I broke my elbow." He grinned. "In high school."

"Your ballistic perception scares me. Yes. In high school."

"I'll borrow a saucepan from Mom," Logan said and headed home to get it.

Vince dialed Brock then talked him into coming over and staying to hang with the teens. Logan returned with his mom, his sister, Maddie, and the pan. Vince put the hot dogs on to boil.

Vince observed Logan's mom chatting personably with Val. For once he experienced thankfulness over Val having the heart to live here. Logan's mom seemed like she could use a good neighbor. And Petrowski's fiancée, Sarah, had been praying for a friend.

It seemed Val was the answer to many prayers.

A strange sensation went through Vince when he recalled Val's suggestion that he had been an answer to people's prayers, too.

Possible? No doubt people prayed when in need of rescue. But his team, not just Vince, was the answer to the prayers of those trapped in peril, right?

Logan's face came to mind.

Had God used Vince in that situation? If so, might He use Vince to help more teens? He eyed Julio and the others. Compassion welled from a cache Vince didn't know was there.

Logan's mom left to do household chores but accepted Val's invitation to return when the food was done.

Vince looked around at all the kids playing in Val's backyard. Hanging in her kitchen. Laughing in her living room. Games and other signs of fun were strewn about. Her home was turned upside down but she didn't seem to care. She seemed only to care about reaching out.

Suddenly he wished he could partner with her in it. That they could serve God together. But in order to do that, Vince had to make peace with God. He'd been so hostile toward God, He might not want Vince.

He checked on the boiling hot dogs then stepped to the window to watch the stunning pink-and-blue sunset. Southern Illinois had some of the most colorful sunsets of anywhere he'd lived. Speaking of stunning…

His gaze tracked Val across the yard. She'd tied a hoodie around her slim waist, and now she went for the ball. She dodged and dribbled and spun and shot.

Whoosh!

She still had it.

And if he wasn't careful, he'd have it for her.

He turned away and flipped the burner off under the frankfurters. Then he set about making slaw and chopping onions. He opened a can of chili and shredded some cheddar cheese. He set things on the counter and decided to spruce up the meal with things he'd learned in cooking school.

Not that he wanted anyone actually knowing that he'd attended school to be a chef, but unfortunately his teammates had found out after Chance had flipped through their mail and happened to see an alumni envelope from the school.

Chance, who never talked, couldn't seem to keep quiet about it to the rest of the team.

And they weren't letting him live it down.

The doorbell rang a little while later, alerting Vince that he'd become too immersed in fancying up the hot dogs.

"Hey, thanks, man." Vince took the new packages of buns from Brock and set them on the table.

Brock set cans of soda in the ice bucket. "Come help me with the grill."

Vince followed him out and they carried the grill to Val's backyard. Logan held open the gate as they came through the side.

Grill fired up, Brock set about methodically laying hamburger patties across it. "Hey, Reardon. You mind separating the frozen ones?"

Val walked up. A fine sheen of sweat covered her skin. Her breathing was a little heavier and her face and neck were flushed from exertion. Her hair looked downright wild.

He loved it.

He cleared his throat and focused on separating the frozen hamburger patties for Brock.

"They wear you out?" Brock asked Val.

She grinned and swigged from her water bottle. "Nearly." She leaned in and sniffed close where Vince stood by Brock who manned the grill. "That smells soooo good."

Vince smirked. "Why, thank you. I take a bath once a month whether I need it or not."

Val laughed. "I meant the burgers."

Brock layered cheese on half of them and Vince scooped them onto a serving platter.

The teens and Val gathered around and dug in to the chips, hot dogs and stack of juicy burgers.

"Logan, did your mom decide not to come back and eat with us?" Val asked.

Logan set his plate aside and surged up. "Oh! I

forgot. She said to come get her whenever the food's done."

"You can phone her instead if you'd like. That's faster than walking down there. Phone's near the fridge."

"'Kay. Thanks." He retreated inside.

"Mmm. Delicious! What did you season those burgers with?" Val asked once she was seated in a lawn chair eating.

Brock lined more patties on the grill and pointed at Vince with tongs. "Ask him. It's his recipe. I'm just the patty turner. He's the accomplished world-class chef."

Val's eyebrows rose. "Reeeeally?"

Vince shot Brock a warning flare. "It's no big deal. You just mix fresh garlic, onion-soup mix and then sprinkle a little Cajun seasoning in the hamburger meat."

Logan came back out with the cordless. "I was on the phone with Mom and someone beeped in. So I clicked over because I didn't want you to miss a call."

Val rose. "Who is it?"

"Someone named Victoria Reardon calling you back."

Vince froze. "Victoria?" Heart pounding and hands quaking with emotion he hadn't realized he'd bottled, he started to rise. Why was she calling? Was something wrong with her or Dad or Mom?

But instead of handing the phone to Vince, Logan handed it to Val.

Color drained from Val's cheeks. She took the phone, darting guilty glances at Vince. Dread filled her face.

Which only confirmed that the person on the other end of his phone was definitely his sister.

Chapter Seventeen

Why was his sister calling Val?

Confusion reached boiling point and anger trailed it. Vince forced himself to sit and act natural since several teens picked up on the exchange.

"Logan, did you say the caller was returning Val's call?" Vince asked discreetly.

"Yeah."

Bigger question: why was Val calling his sister?

Serious tension and a sickening sense of betrayal twisted his neck into knots.

Speaking quietly, Val stepped indoors. Vince had half a mind to follow her. If that was indeed his sister, and not some girl with the same name, he had every right to know what this was about.

Had they been in contact before? Were they friends? Had his sister spewed stories of their difficult childhood? Had Val only befriended Vince out of pity?

The thought made him want to crush the basket-ball. He restrained his emotions until Val could explain herself.

She returned. "Vince, may I have a word with you?"

He rose, trying, like Val, to act as if nothing was wrong. But something was very wrong. He saw it in Val's eyes. How had Vic gotten Val's unlisted number? Or known he was here? That she didn't ask for Vince seared like an RPG.

Val wrung her hands as she closed the door behind them. "I know that was a shock."

"So it *was* my sister."

"Yes. But I can explain."

"Not now." He eyed the door. "Long as she wasn't calling to say someone's dead or dying, I'm not ready to hear it. Not in front of the kids."

"Okay. Everything's fine."

The want to know overpowered his vow of tem-porary silence. "Then why'd she call you?"

"I contacted her because I felt bad about the bike. I wish I could say more but I promised I wouldn't. Everyone in your family is safe and sound."

"I wouldn't call Dad sound. But, whatever. Look, let's just go back in there and act normal." Tension crackled between them but they rejoined the teens.

"I didn't realize you were such a good cook, Vince," Val said as the group gathered for a lavish dessert.

Brock snorted. "He didn't tell you he studied abroad to be a chef, huh?"

Spoon to her mouth, Val looked up. "Is he kidding?"

Vince kicked Brock beneath the table. "Unfortunately not."

Logan stood. "Dude! You're a famous chef? That is so cool."

"I'm not famous by any means." Vince filled his plate.

"I bet you could be. Hey, you could have your own reality show," a teen girl said.

"Yeah, it could be called *Parachutes and Veggie Shoots*," Julio said.

Val laughed. *"Rip Cords and Garnished Gourds."*

"Lemonades and Hand Grenades." Brock snorted.

"Bakery Boot Camp," another teen said.

"Or *Soufflés and Maroon Berets.*" Julio cackled.

Vince laughed then grew serious. "Hey, wait. How'd you know we wear maroon berets?"

The tall kid dipped his head. Shrugged. "Looked it up online." He met Vince's gaze with uncharacteristic respect. "You PJs are cool. What you do is insane but awesome. Risking your skin to rescue. That's pretty amazing."

"Stay out of trouble and quit bullying people, and your life can count for something, too," Vince said.

"You think? Shut *up!* I'll never amount to nothing but trouble."

Vince wasn't offended by the "shut up" because he'd figured out it was a slangy compliment of sorts. "Who says you won't amount to anything?"

Julio's chair creaked. "My old man."

"Well, your dad's a first-class smart—"

"Vince. Young ears." Her fingers had covered his mouth in much the same way they had her mom's earlier.

Vince curbed his urge to use the expletive around the teens. "You can amount to whatever you set your mind to."

"He means God has a plan for your life if you'd like to take hold of it."

"I dig hanging around you two. You always make me feel like my life could really matter someday."

Vince knuckled his head. "It could. And you know why?"

"Because you matter to God," Val finished.

Julio looked like he wanted to believe it. Vince hoped like crazy the kid didn't end up disappointed.

"Guys, let's go pick up outside." Brock rose and led the teens out to clean up cups and plates.

Vince watched them clean up. His gaze tracked Julio and Logan.

Val stood beside him. "They remind you of yourself at that age?"

"In different ways."

"I'm sorry, Vince."

His jaw clenched. "I don't need your pity, Val. It won't right the wrongs."

Difficult memories dropped into Vince's mind like an unexpected enemy insurgence. Memories of hope that had been deferred when his desperate prayers had gone unheard or at least unanswered. When he was young and crying out for his dad to stop drowning himself in the bottle.

And again when attorneys in court would not listen to his brother plead his innocence and for his freedom.

He thought Val was different. Until he'd gotten whiffs of her going behind his back and being secretive.

Memories tore into the canopy that had sheltered him from doubt that plagued his life since those dark days.

And reinforced his initial perception: that all attorneys, Val included, were underhanded in some way.

At what point had he made the mistake and begun hoping she'd be the exception?

"With rare exception, where peace is concerned, things get worse right before they get better. That's the nature of warfare."

Val watched the military documentary commentator on TV with Sarah a week and a day after the youth bash. A huge bowl of popcorn sat on the couch between them.

"It astounds me how many similarities physical warfare has with spiritual." Val sipped her soda. Tea never tasted right with popcorn. Especially during movies with a friend.

"Now that you mention it, I agree. Heard from Vince yet?"

"No. I don't even know if he still wants me to go to the PJ cookout this evening."

"I'm inviting you."

"Do you know why it was cancelled last Saturday? Because Vince was a no-show for church on Sunday, too."

"I'm not supposed to tell you this, but I think I can trust you not to say anything. Vince didn't stand you up. They were called away on an emergency mission."

"In the States?"

"No. Not a civilian rescue. Something military. High-profile. I'm pretty sure it was a pilot rescue. Only, things didn't go as planned."

"Is everyone okay?"

"Mostly. There were problems with radios being programmed into the wrong code. And they were almost captured by the militants."

Val rose, hand to her throat. "Nearly captured?"

"Yes, two allied pilots were shot down in Afghanistan. One survived. One did not. The guys are all pretty bummed over it."

"Do they lose pilots often?"

"Rarely, but that they almost lost teammates made this rescue worse. Look, I really shouldn't tell you more."

"I'm sorry for pressing you."

"No, it's not that. It's just…Vince is who programmed the radios wrong. It was a huge error that almost cost the team their lives."

Val gasped. "Is he in trouble for it?"

"No. Joel and Petrowski aren't like that. Commanders above tried to eat Vince for lunch, but Aaron convinced them he'd bring disciplinary action against him."

"What did he do?"

"Ordered Vince to a curfew and sentenced him to seven hours of sleep per night. Severe sleep deprivation probably caused the error."

"I'm glad it wasn't something harsh."

"As Petrowski put it, love covers a multitude of sins."

"I'll bet Vince feels terrible."

"He's the worst I've ever seen him. Totally down in the dumps. He doesn't feel worthy to be part of the team anymore. That's probably why you haven't heard from him."

"He left the youth bash angrier than a volcano because I contacted his sister. It erupted all kinds of molten memories regarding the injustice surrounding his brother's death."

"God must really be working on him. Vince must be getting close to giving in. Otherwise the enemy wouldn't be fighting so hard to keep him."

"I hope you're right."

"You care about him, don't you?"

"More than I ought. Maybe this sudden change in Vince isn't the enemy at all. Maybe this is God redirecting me because my heart's the one that got too close."

"I don't know the answer."

"Either way, I'd be better off to stick around here tonight rather than go to the cookout."

"Sure?"

"Yeah. I'll go another time. Elsie's not here again this weekend and her bird gets scared of storms. I hate to leave him, even though he bites."

"Hmm. Sounds like Vince."

Val laughed.

Sarah eyed her watch. "I need to meet Aaron and the boys before the cookout. Sure you don't want to come?"

"No, I need to pray through this storm." Pray for Vince, too, rather than be mad at him for flaking on church.

Remorse sucked her insides out for being oblivious to considering that Vince might be struggling.

Val unfolded her legs from underneath her and walked Sarah to the door.

"It's already starting to rain. Looks like Aaron will have to move the cookout into the pole barn."

"Have fun. Bye, Sarah."

Val locked the door and shut her blinds. Fed the bird. Cleaned out his bowl. "Why do you poop and sleep in the same place that you eat? That's really gross." Maybe she should clean out his cage and his food container before she prayed.

Truth be known, she was avoiding the Bible and prayer, fearing God might tell her to pull away from Vince because she'd let her heart get entangled.

She eyed her Bible. Eyed the bird's dish. Eyed her Bible. And reached for the dish. Then settled on her couch with a fashion magazine. Flipped through it. Set it aside. Stretched. Turned on the TV. Watched three minutes of a talk show that shouldn't have made her laugh.

"Squawk box." She poked the remote at the TV and powered it off.

"Hi, Pretty Bad Boy. Hi, Pretty Bad Boy. Hi, Pretty Boy."

Val groaned at the bird who always said that phrase to Vince and only Vince whenever he walked in.

"Hi, Pretty Bad Boy. Hi, Pretty Bad Boy. Hiiigh." He preened his feathers and puffed out his chest and swung his torso back and forth and side to side on the perch.

"You be quiet. He's not here."

"Hi, Pretty Bad Boooyy."

"Grrr!" She aimed the remote at the bird and pressed Pause multiple times, hoping for silence.

No go.

"Shush! You're a squawk box, too."

A loud thump on her porch and a scraping knock caused the remote to slip from her fingers. "Oh!"

Another strange tap. She peeped through the view hole in the door. Vince. Looking wet and haggard.

She eyed her watch. Late. Hours past the cookout. She opened the door. "What's wrong?" she asked. He hunched his shoulders from the rain. "I need somebody to talk to." Rain pelted his face much the way it had that day in the road. And the raw look also resided in his eyes. She swung open the door.

"Come in." She grabbed a towel from the bathroom.

He took it and wiped his face. "Thanks."

"Have a seat."

Vince folded the towel on the couch and sat on it.

Val brought him a glass of tea the way he liked it. Sipping her own, she sat beside him. "What's going on?"

He shrugged. Stared into the glass. "Sarah tell you?"

Gulp. "She might have mentioned it."

"Val, please. Be straight with me."

"She told me about the radios." She reached out her hand. "Vince, no one's mad at you."

"Yeah, but did she tell you about the freaky stuff?"

"I— Maybe—I'm not sure what you mean."

He scooted forward on the couch. "I tried to drink tonight. To avoid stuff. Couldn't."

"Couldn't avoid stuff?"

"No, couldn't drink. I stared into the glass and it hit me like a flash-bang. I stared at the liquid and knew that was the poison killing my dad. I'm done."

"Drinking?"

"Yes, and more. I'm done running. Look, it's late. If you're tired—"

She put her hand on his arm.

Bad move.

He stared at it, then at her. Gazes locked, they drifted toward one another. Who embraced who first, she couldn't be sure.

His cheek rested against hers, his warm breath near her mouth. "Val, there's so much I wanna tell you but, because it's classified, I can't. But it's about the mission."

Her heart leaped. His arms tightened around her.

"No way can I deny there was something beyond human intervention out there. Had Joel and Aaron not been leaders who pray, Val, I don't think our team would have made it home. And it would have been my fault."

"But no one blames you."

"I don't know how. I don't understand that kind of mercy. But I want to. Joel said it's only a speck compared to the mercy God has toward us. Is that true?"

"Yes. His mercies are new every day. Like the sunrise, you can depend on it rising up. But unlike the sun, God's mercy doesn't disappear in dark seasons."

He nodded. "Before this mission, that never woulda made sense to me."

"I'm glad it's making sense now." He cuddled her close. He shifted his face so his mouth glided over hers in the softest, sweetest kiss. A kiss with purity and promise.

He pulled away before Val. Brushed hair from her eyes and planted another kiss on her forehead. "I want to stay but I need to go."

"Yeah. Elsie's not here to chaperone."

Vince chuckled and gave her shoulders another squeeze. He tugged her up from the couch and she walked him to the door. "What's so funny? Why the big grin?"

At the doorway, his gaze grew a little bolder as he brushed it over her face and locked it onto her lips. "I wonder."

Heat rushed her cheeks. She started to dip her face, but his fingers lifted her chin. He bent to kiss her again and this one bordered on electric. By the time he pulled away, her lips and her brain tingled. "Bye, Vince."

He backed off the porch, holding on to her fingers. Their arms extended as he backed away until their fingers slipped from one another's hands. "G'night, Miss Distraction."

"Night, Pretty Boy."

He paused. "Don't you mean Bad Boy?"

She shook her head. "I'm making a motion to switch your identity with that of Squawk Box. From now on, he's Bad Boy and you're Pretty. And you are, in a rugged kind of way."

Vince smirked. "Yeah, well don't tell the guys that or I'll deny it to the death."

She laughed and let him go, not wanting to risk, wanting to beg him back in. He held her gaze as he stepped backward off her porch, smiling like he had a secret.

She slipped back and firmly closed her door.

Then went to the window and watched him pull out in Chance's truck. At least he had sense enough not to ride in the rain this time.

The next weeks could be the most crucial in Vince's life. God was actively recruiting, she was sure of that.

What she wasn't sure of was how Vince would react to the divine pursuant. Whether he rode away or toward remained to be seen.

Chapter Eighteen

"Ready to ride?"

Val's cheeks heated at the deep rumble near her left ear. Joy at hearing his voice brought an instant smile. She turned to face Vince, dressed in skydiving gear. "Hey, Pretty Boy," she said, low.

"Hey, watch it." He winked and looked over her shoulder at the other PJs rustling around the DZ.

The urge to hug him hello accosted her.

"Be right back." He passed casually with a parachute pack in his arms. He cradled it as carefully as if it were an infant. A swift, powerful image flashed across Val's mind of Vince holding a real baby. Longing swept through her to have a marriage and a family with him.

With great effort, she bottled the hope trying to stream out like strands of bubbles blown by wedding guests.

Unless she had more evidence he shared her faith, the yearning did not deserve to be dwelled on.

He returned looking more serene than she'd seen him in weeks. "Did you drop by just to see me?" His grin widened.

Brock passed. "Don't blow his head up, Val. Deny it."

Val laughed. "Actually, Sarah had to stop by here and pick something up. So seeing you was an unexpected surprise." A nice one.

He looked even more inviting and intriguing in his bright jumpsuit and military skydiving gear.

Val tucked a lock of hair behind her ears and glanced at Sarah, who winked and walked toward the door to greet Aaron. Val turned back to Vince. "Thought you said you'd be late."

"Figured we would be. But the thought of seeing you made me get my work done faster." He grinned.

She let her smile at that fade. "Vince, we need to talk."

"I know." Sincerity sparkled in eyes so intense she couldn't look away. He had the kind of eyes that hardly blinked through the most prolonged eye contact of anyone she knew.

Positioning his torso toward her, he continued to look carefully at her as he handed his pack to Chance, who reached for it on his way to the back room.

"Thanks," he said to Chance, who grinned at Val from ear to ear. Vince never removed his gaze from Val. The wattage on his grin turned up slightly, as though he waited for her to notice something.

She studied him like a set of evidence, then looked around her. Peripherally, she caught his smile explode.

In fact, Vince's entire team was grinning ear to ear.

Turning back, Val eyed Vince carefully. He seemed different somehow. Lighter. She tilted her head. "What's going on, Vince?"

He stood with his feet slightly apart, hands casually turning something in his hands. "I lied to you. I didn't get any work done today."

"You didn't?" She eyed the object being transferred from one hand to the other. The motion mesmerized her.

The box looked suspiciously like a jeweler's gift box.

She raised her attention from it to his face. For the first time, Vince broke eye contact with her to stare over her shoulder. A look of deep satisfaction caused his features to sober and a thankful expression coated his face as he gave a slight nod to whoever was approaching behind her. Val inclined her head as the person passed. Joel.

He answered Vince's nod with one of his own and walked by looking about to implode with joy. "No, he did something far more important." Joel's voice thickened with emotion as words tumbled out in excited tones.

As Joel passed, he clamped a hand on Vince's shoulder and squeezed. "Tell her, bud."

Val eyed Vince. "What's different about you?

What happened today?" Hope rose in her heart at the light and peace in his eyes.

Vince motioned toward the parking lot. "Let's go for a walk. It's sunny outside for the first time in my life."

She followed him in a state of wonder. What was different about him? Even his walk seemed different. His entire demeanor. Hope and tears of the possibility, the thing she hoped it to be, flooded to the surface.

They walked leisurely side by side around three-quarters of the parking lot before Vince said another word.

Near a patio with a wrought-iron table and chairs, he stopped and drew an eternal breath. "I've been asking some hard questions." He pulled a chair out for her.

Val sat. "About?"

He rested his hands on the back of the opposite chair. "God."

"To Joel?"

He shook his head. "No. Well, some. But mostly to God."

Her mouth fell open. "You've been praying?"

He waved his hand. "Well, if that's what you want to call it."

"Vince!" She surged from the chair and plowed into him, hugging with all her might. "Vince, this is—"

"Not the end of what I need to say." His arms

wound around her but only for a moment. Not nearly long enough. He held back. Why? He motioned her to keep walking.

She tamped down her excitement and fell into step beside him.

After a moment, he drew another sustaining breath. "Val, I need you to know that I'm not doing this for you. This seeking of Him. I have to figure out things for myself. You know, if He's all you guys say He's cracked up to be. Then, well, I asked Him to show me."

Val's heart pounded. Especially when Vince flicked what looked suspiciously like a tear away. "My sister called me the very next day. So did my old man. Granted, he was drunk as usual, but—" Vince swallowed hard twice before words would come. "He told me something he's never said."

"What?" Val's voice felt as raw as Vince's sounded.

"Told me he loved me. And that he wanted a relationship with me. Told me that he'd try to quit drinking if Victoria and I would try to reconcile."

Val took Vince's hand. "Fabulous!"

He shrugged and paused to look at her. "I'll be honest. I'm still working through some anger."

"At Victoria? Or your dad?"

"No. At the courts because they killed my brother."

"I agree that was a gross miscarriage of justice."

"I'm also still ticked because you went behind my back and messed with things that were none of your business." Though his words sliced out with edge, his smile returned.

"You're still uproariously peeved about that, aren't you?"

The forthright sarcasm she'd been missing returned to his expression. "That depends."

"On?"

"Whether you're going to continue to meddle in my life uninvited."

Steps slowed, she dipped her head. "I know. I'm sorry. I went about it the wrong way."

Also pausing, he brought his hand to her face. Stepped close. Closer. His finger curved under her chin and lifted it so they were eye to eye. "But it just so happens that your saving grace is that Victoria e-mailed me some sleek and sexy photos she took. They curbed my anger toward you."

"What pictures?"

"Of the new bike she's been building since those phone calls you finagled."

Val shot a triumphant fist in the air. "Yes!" She jerked her arm down. "Oh, wait. You're still grumpy because I called her."

He tugged a curvaceous bottom lip between gleaming white teeth.

"What if I invited you?"

"To meddle?" Her voice rose.

His lowered. "And more."

"What does that mean?"

"I know that you don't want to live like Elsie lived.

You deserve someone man enough to run hard after God *for* God and no other reason."

She nodded.

"Val, I so badly want to be that man. But—"

Ecstatic tears burned her eyes. She swallowed against the urge to shriek with joy.

His knuckle swabbed the tear streaking down her face. "I don't know if I ever can. You know, live up to that."

She took his strong hands in hers. "Vince, you can. The main thing is to ensure that nothing competes with devotion to Jesus. That you already know that on your own speaks well of your motives and smacks of success."

An instant grin split his face. "Hey, you just said street slang. Nice job, Miss Distraction. I can tell you've been studying up on urban lingo."

"And I can tell He's doing a mighty work in your heart. You've come so far." She squeezed his hands.

He squeezed back. His thumbs kneaded the ball of flesh between the webbing of her thumb and first finger, sending a tingling up her arm.

"By the way, I got the letter from the courts about my brother's name being officially cleared. Thanks for expediting that." A reminiscent gleam entered his eyes. "I grew up unchurched. Dad used the only Bible in the house for a beer coaster. He was a soft-workin', hard-drinkin' Irishman. Mom was a hot-blooded Italian."

"I wondered about your ancestry. Now I know

where you inherited your temper. I bet you get the dark, Italian looks from your mom and the Irish surname courtesy of your father."

"Yeah. She's still firing up dance floors in Vegas. He lives in a quaint little drinking village that has a fishing problem."

She laughed out loud. "Is that so?"

"Yeah. Homer, Alaska. Even the town sign says so." He tilted his head. "Your eyes just lit up."

"That's because I got an idea."

Now his eyes lit up. "Is it devious?"

"Can you not be nice for five minutes?"

"Five whole minutes?" He made a show of looking pained.

She smacked his arm. "Do you want to hear my proposition or not?"

"You're proposing?" The teasing, flirty glint that she'd been missing orbited back into his eyes.

Took her a second to look away. "Will you be serious for two seconds so I can state my case?" She laughed.

He chopped a salute to his forehead. "Ma'am, yes, ma'am. Order in the court."

"My idea will benefit both of us."

"So, you're negotiating a plea bargain here."

"Sorta. Actually, yes. Guilty as charged. Anyway, how about you teach me how to cook and I will teach you stories from the Bible." She steeled herself for his oral afterburners to blast her idea to infinity.

The explosion never came. She loosened her

shoulders and peeked up at him. "Mercy. You are actually thinking about it. Aren't you?"

"About as hard as you were thinking about proposing." He crossed his arms over his chest.

She took his hand and unfurled his arms. "Who said I wasn't thinking about it?"

"You're too old-fashioned to ask a man to marry you."

She smiled inside, knowing that if he truly gave his heart one hundred percent to God, she'd propose in the next heartbeat.

"Fine," he said.

Chapter Nineteen

"Fine?" Her head whipped around. The most shocked expression came across her face as her jaw slackened. "Fine?" She repeated his phrasing and blinked.

"Don't look so confused, Val. I'm agreeing to the plea bargain."

"You're really going to let me teach you about the Bible?"

"Yes. If you promise to stay away from your oven buttons unless Refuge's fire department has been notified to be on standby. I mean it. No touching the burn controls on your stove either."

"And what about church?"

"I offered to go. You forbid me." He smirked.

She gasped. "I didn't want you to feel coerced or—"

"Val." He put his hand on her arm. "I'm kidding. I'll give church a shot this weekend."

"You're really serious."

"I'm really serious." And frightened out of his gourd. Because once he gave his word, he didn't go back on it. "But you have to let me teach you how to cook anything I choose." He unleashed his most wicked grin.

Her smile evaporated and her eyes bulged. "Anything?"

"Anything."

"When?"

"We'll start tonight. I'll give you lessons several times a week. Then once you grow comfortable, I'll step up your cooking lessons by teaching you how to master the mammoth grill for the PJ cookout."

"Vince! I can't cook for all those people!"

"If I can go be trapped in a creepy steepled building for two hours with a bunch of churchy people, then, yes, you can."

"This church has no steeple. It's a pole barn like the DZ. The same contractor designed both buildings. And the people aren't churchy. They're very casual and laid-back. It's a jeans-on-Sunday kind of place. Think of your teammates. Joel. Ben. Aaron. Nolan. Are they churchy?"

"No, but that's different. Anyway, after the grill sessions and cookouts, you can teach me how to master the Good News."

"How do you know that's what it's called?"

"Told you. I've been asking questions."

Back at the DZ lot, he motioned her toward his

bike. "Come on, Miss Distraction. I have some teens to pick up."

"Logan mentioned you'd invited him and some of the other guys to the cookout."

"Yeah. I hope my team will inspire them to make something out of themselves other than inmates."

The bike's weight shifted as Val climbed on behind him. Felt good to have her close again. Things felt good, period. Better than they had in a long time.

And, not that he was ready to admit it out loud yet, but deep down he knew his improved outlook on life had more to do with God than with the girl.

He revved the engine and ate up the highway until they arrived at Val's place. He cut the engine to find her laughing.

"What's so funny?" He helped her off the bike.

She pulled her blue helmet off. "I just realized I never said goodbye to Sarah."

"She'll understand. She's fallen in love before."

Val's mouth dropped open. "Just how do you know I—"

"Because I can read you like a Miranda Right. Come on, Miss Distraction."

Several teens exited yards and houses and meandered toward Val's as had become the custom anytime Vince's bike rumbled through the neighborhood.

"I love that you love your home to be the hangout place." Vince walked toward the approaching group.

Val followed, waving at parents in yards. "Elsie's gift of hospitality wore off on me. She babysat me growing up."

"I'm glad for the impact you're making on these families by living among them." He suspected she'd befriended many of the mothers. Or tried to.

Vince shook macho handshakes with the teen boys while the girls followed Val like chicks trailing a mother hen into the house.

Once in the house, Vince, chuckling, followed Val to the mirror in her hallway near the bathroom to fix her wild helmet hair.

Once out of earshot of the teens, he whistled low and made a cat call. "It's edgy kinda wild." He brushed a hand along the hairline above her ear and let his fingers graze along her jawline, lifting only when they happened upon the hollow of her neck.

A flush colored her cheeks. "I'm far from edgy. And the only one of us around here who's wild is you." She turned her face to the side and finger-straightened her unruly mess of hair.

He leaned closer, spanning his hands around her waist. "I'm tamed. The only way I am still wild…is about you."

For a second she swayed as though to lean into him for a stolen kiss, then cleared her throat and wrenched herself from his reach. "Vince, young eyes are watching."

He turned to find Logan grinning at them from the end of the hall. Vince reluctantly let her go and sauntered toward Logan, whose grin ratcheted up with every step.

"I knew it." Logan smirked.

"What?"

"Don't play dumb. You guys are into each other."

Vince eyed Val. "Yeah, but some things have to line up first. So keep it under your Mohawk."

Logan grinned. "Sure. So what's the holdup?"

"I had some decisions to make. Needed to make sure they took."

"Like what?" Logan looked like he really wanted to know. Vince felt connected enough with the kid to tell.

"I—you know—prayed for Him to be my God."

Logan's eyes bugged. "Seriously? When?"

"After a near-deadly mission that almost went from rescue to recovery. I prayed a few times, actually."

"Dude, when was this?"

"Let's see." Vince counted on his fingers. "Once in a car trunk. Again on a dusty hundred-and-twenty-degree Afghanistan road running for my life with tanks on our tail. Once with my team when fleeing for the border with RPGs whizzing over our heads. Then again when I realized He intervened to save my team despite a morose mistake on my part."

Logan laughed. "That'll do it." He eyed Val, who rejoined the group of teens settled around her living room. "She know?"

Vince shook his head. "Not yet. I want to be sure I'm really doing it for Him and not her."

"Dude, there's no doubt in my mind that it did. You're way different. And I mean that in a good way."

"Thanks, Logan. That means a lot."

"So when you gonna tell her?"

As though sensing his gaze on her, Val sought then found his face.

He eyed her with the fondness he felt inside. "Soon." Vince shrugged. "When I get the courage to eat my crow. Because once I tell her, she's gonna wanna tell Joel and Petrowski and the others."

Logan laughed. "And knowing those guys, they're gonna wanna say *I told you so.*"

"Yeah. I mean, they kinda know I'm seeking, but they don't know I already decided. I'm just sorta basking in the time with Him. Like it's our secret. Once it's out, they won't let me live it down. Especially Brock and Chance."

Logan shook his head. "I think they'll be too happy to gloat. Besides, the sooner it comes out, the sooner she can stop holding back."

"Logan, how'd you get to be so smart?"

"Mom. But don't tell her I told you that. It's amazing how the older I get the smarter Mom seems."

Vince laughed. "In some cases. Unless the kids outclass the parents in maturity and responsibility."

"Yeah, dude, I'm sorry. I keep forgetting you had a rough go at it, too."

"It's all right. Things are getting better. I've been talking more to my dad."

"For what it's worth, I think all that stuff you went through as a kid will make you a phenomenal dad."

"Is that right?"

"Yeah, and if you didn't have eyes for Miss Distraction over there, I'd seriously try to hook you up with my mom."

"Hey, for the record, in case there's speculation among your peers, Val and I aren't hooking up. Not in the way most young people think of it nowadays."

"Yeah, I figured that." Logan grinned. "We know you're the kind of adults who do what you say and live like you mean it." Logan struck a cool pose as a group of girls passed to enter the bathroom.

Vince laughed and motioned Logan back to join the games. "Let's see what everyone's up to." Some teens clustered around Val's computer, uploading pictures.

Vince walked past the counter and Val, on the phone now, scratched notes on her legal pad. "Okay. Yes. I will. Yep. That's what you need to do. Because at this point everything is circumstantial. So we'll have to figure out how to trip the weakest witness up."

Vince paused, a sick feeling roiling inside. Sick because he'd intentionally progressed things romantically with them. Sweet kisses. Lingering looks. Soft touches—subtle, modest, yet enough to get his point across that he wanted to stake his claim on her as a man. He wanted her to be his. And he wanted it for life.

Life.

Circumstantial. Weak witnesses. Trip them up.

Exactly what happened to his brother.

She was still an attorney. And from the way she'd talked just then, the kind of attorney who'd deceive a jury to defend their case regardless of whether the accused was guilty or innocent. Finally sensing his nearness, she angled her torso toward him and gave his forearm a friendly squeeze. Vince recoiled.

Her smile faded. Val completed her call and faced Vince. "Hey, what's wrong?" Her forehead crinkled.

"Who was on the phone?"

"A colleague. Why?"

"Sounds like you were talking shop."

"We were. Have a big case next week."

Fury pressed past the threshold of his patience and hurtled through him. "A case with no hard evidence."

Her face flushed then paled. "Vince, it's not like that." She stepped toward him. He stepped back just as fast. "Don't come near."

Don't come near.

Val's heart sank. Because his words meant more than physical proximity. His walls had sprung up again. Swift. Impenetrable.

"How can you call yourself a Christian and manipulate someone's future for selfish gain?"

"Vince, I—"

He shook his head. Slow. Methodical. Fiercely angry. "Whatever it is, save it."

"Listen, for a—"

"No, Val. Nothing you can say will bring my brother back or change the fact that lies and circumstantial evidence put him in the grave."

Logan wandered in and stopped dead in his tracks. "Everything okay?"

A shadow passed over Vince's face, but he camouflaged calm into his expression as he turned his back to Val in order to face Logan. "Yeah. But I need to jet, and you all promised to obey our curfews."

"Ah, bummer. We wanted to hang out more."

"Another time." Vince scrubbed a fist over Logan's head and approached the rest of the group.

Val followed stiffly, feeling numb like a bomb had just gone off inside her, obliterating her motor skills.

The hurt and anger that had flashed like fire from Vince still seared fresh in her mind.

How would he ever get past the pain? And could he ever accept her career so things could progress romantically as he was progressing in his faith walk?

She observed Vince's body language the way she did witnesses and clients in court. Thankfully for the teens, he gave off no cues or clues that anything was wrong. She should be angry. She should be caring to defend herself since he'd accused her of something terrible. But instead, peace befell her. *Thank You.*

Val couldn't stand the pain in his eyes. Unresolved anguish. "Vince, can you help me get something from the top of the cabinet?" She tugged him into her laundry room.

His lips compressed into a hard line. "You don't really need me to reach anything."

"No. I pulled you in here because I need to reach you."

He started for the door. She grabbed his arm. "Vince, please. Hear me out."

He paused. Faced her.

Give me words that will make a difference.

"Please trust me. Trust what you know of me and don't base your assumptions of me on past experiences. I will not prosecute anyone without solid evidence. This client has a history of perjuring himself in court. Please choose to believe that there is more good in the system than bad. Most good guys do go free."

"Not my brother." This time pain resided in his eyes more than anger. And the pain was pliable.

But Val's words had at least snapped the soft side of him back to attention. It also proved to her that God was working in Vince's heart, too, and that Vince was at least a little open to it.

Thank You.

"We need to get out of here before the kids get the wrong idea. You first." Vince sent her out, then he came out a few minutes later so it didn't seem they were in there at the same time.

"You guys coming to the PJ cookout?" Vince asked the teens as they got ready to head home for curfews.

Most of them said they were. Vince had yet to talk

Julio into hanging with the guys. But he looked like he wanted to go. "You know you're welcome, right?"

He shrugged. "I'll think about it."

"Fair enough." Vince made eye contact with Val and the usual connection wasn't only back but stronger.

Not just the deep, loving care and understanding between them, but their unified care for the teens and the joint determination to make a difference in their lives.

She would fight the unseen enemies for this man. No doubt she could let herself love him since his heart was now firmly God's.

Vince held the door open as the last teens filed out and scattered in huddles of two or three down the sidewalks flanking Val's yard.

As always, after each youth bash, they'd stand on the porch and keep every teen in sight until sure they all made it safely inside their homes.

"Darkness is descending earlier."

With the last teen blinking her porch light to signal she was inside and all was well, Vince not only faced Val but pulled her fully into his arms and held firmly.

"But not even the darkest night seems so black lately." His throat muscles tightened above her forehead, evidence of emotion his voice wouldn't let him expound.

But he didn't have to finish for her to know he meant since God's hope for a brighter future had surfaced on his horizon.

Chapter Twenty

"That's one way to get them to go," Val said Sunday morning as Vince picked them up in the rickety rented bus.

Vince pulled out onto the street. "Bribing them with ice cream at Cone Zone? Yeah, brilliant." He laughed.

"Is Brock going?"

"I suspect he's riding with Chance who, along with the rest of the town, will no doubt show up at church just to see if I actually go through with it."

Val laughed and adjusted her seat belt.

"Ay! Hands in the air, Julio," Vince said into the wide rearview mirror. The girl beside him blushed.

Julio muttered a groan but lifted his hands. "Dude, you putting me under arrest on Sunday?"

"Yes. In fact, I'm putting you in a different seat." Vince pulled over to a curb along the street in front of the abandoned skating rink. "Move it."

Val eyed Julio's new girlfriend, a different one

from yesterday, who slunk down in the seat and rolled her eyes.

Vince slid a glance at Val. "Trust me. I was his age once."

She laughed and held her hands up. "I didn't say a word."

"I know the kinds of things that go on behind green seats." Vince scanned the mirror for clandestine activity. *Watched like a military surveillance device* more described the hawkish look in his heart-melting eyes.

"For what it's worth, I think you'd be a great dad. And if she were my daughter, I'd be thankful to have a leader like you in her life. You're a great role model."

"Now. Not back then. Not only was I once exactly Julio's age, I was exactly his type."

She shared a laugh, then Vince's smile grew thoughtful. "Four kids, huh? Not at the same time I hope." He slid a sideways glance her way.

A nervous laugh scraped up her throat and her cheeks heated. "No, not at the same time. Can you imagine?"

Vince eyed the teen drama and nail-polish pande-monium in the back of the bus. "Yes. Which is what terrifies me." He laughed and turned on some modern edgy music and the kids sang popular songs the rest of the way to church.

"How'd you get Julio and Logan to come?"

Vince laughed. "Told them that misery loved

company. And said since I had to go, the three of us may as well suffer through it together."

Val laughed. "Oh, the trauma."

"Hey, as Joel says, whatever it takes."

"Whatever it takes. And for the record, where you're concerned, I'm glad it took." She reached for his hand on the shifter.

"Hey! Watch it up there. We'll separate you two," Julio called out. The entire bus snickered and snorted.

Val rolled her eyes and slid her hand from Vince's. "Nothing like a dozen nosey chaperones."

Vince grinned. "We can drop 'em off in a ditch anytime you're ready."

She laughed. "Not hardly. Behave yourself."

"I'm trying. Trust me. It's not easy where you're concerned." He gave her red skirt and exposed lower legs an appreciative glance that set her face ablaze. "And for what it's worth, you'd be a phenomenal mom."

She studied him, surprised to see his ears shading red. He shifted in his seat and set his gaze back on the road. "And—" he cleared his throat "—I think to that end, we'd make a great team."

She grinned widely. "I love you, too, Vince."

"Who says I love you?" He flicked a teasing glint at her before returning his attention to finding a parking spot as he entered Refuge Community Church's lot.

"Mostly, your charm and your charms."

He grinned to match hers. "Well, since all the experts say that chicks need to hear it from men's mouths and not just their motives, then here goes. I love you, Val."

She snorted. "Not exactly romantic with a dozen noisy beings bouncing around a bus, but I'll gladly take it."

He held her hand as they walked in. Chance and Brock, along with Vince's entire team, were lined up like sentries at the church door. Joel's face lit when he saw that Vince had actually shown. Vince's heart warmed at the deep care embedded in the eyes of each of these men for one another.

They were like a family. A brotherhood.

Once all the teens were inside, thanks to PJs Ben and Nolan who worked with the youth program, Vince pulled Val near a decorative tree at the side of the building.

"Are you nervous?" He wasn't chickening out, was he?

"Nope." He removed his sunglasses, pulled her into his arms and kissed the common sense right out of her. Her legs turned to rubber as he ended the sweet but sultry kiss and peered down at her. "I love you. And that's the best way I know to show it."

She gulped. "Do me a favor. Don't show me you love me too many more times until we make it legal."

He laughed and tugged her toward the door. "Come on. We're running late. The music's starting."

She tugged him back. "Yes, it's just begun. And by the way, you big, brooding hunk of a brute, I love you, too."

"I know." He smiled and pulled his shades on as they walked into the building. Why did that sunglass action not surprise her? Probably for the same reason her proclamation didn't seem to surprise him.

Because they knew one another deeply. She reminisced about the claim-staking kiss and his words of devotion and sighed with a contentment and peace she hadn't felt in years.

Vince sat quietly through the service. His face and body remained utterly unreadable. At least he was leaning forward, in active-listening mode, instead of storming out, as he might have done a few months ago when he wasn't ready.

That he didn't go forward during the invitation didn't bother Val, because she knew he said he'd prayed alone for Jesus to come in His heart and be his God. His salvation was secure. God would disciple Vince in His own time frame.

Ben Dillinger led the church in one last authentic worship song with his acoustic guitar, with lyrics he'd composed, while a ministry team prayed for people up front.

Afterward, the pastor dismissed the service and people began filing out of rows. Vince sat quietly in deep thought.

After a moment, he tilted his head toward her and, in a peaceful voice, said, "I'm glad Julio and Logan came. I like the way that guy teaches." He viewed the pastor.

"Are you glad *you* came?"

He grinned. "I just came for the coffee and to be able to sit by a hot girl."

She rolled her eyes and shooed him from the aisle. "Leave it to the bad boy to lie in church."

He raised his chin and laughed heartily. "I seriously do need a cup of joe."

Val motioned the kids in the direction of the refreshment area.

A rough-looking man intercepted them between the sanctuary and the lobby en route to the coffee lounge. Val might have mistaken him for one of Vince's party buddies except that she'd seen him both leading and engaging in worship.

Her first Sunday at Refuge visiting Refuge Community Church she'd sat behind him, admittedly mesmerized by the Mohawk, tattoos and heavily pierced man in ripped-up jeans lifting his hands and face to God and singing his heart out.

She'd had to force herself to focus on God and not the people around her. But she'd decided that day that this was to be her church home because she would feel comfortable bringing the teens here.

Vince moved closer to Val as the man approached. He did that a lot when another guy turned attention her way. But this man's attention fell only briefly on her before bypassing to rest firmly on Vince. He had hospitable drivenness, a missional intensity about him.

He looked at Vince like he knew him, yet seemed unsure. He reached out his hand. "Hi, my name's Rowan Cline. You don't happen to be a Reardon, do you?"

Vince stiffened. He issued a stiff handshake, too. "Matter of fact, I am. What's it to you?"

The young inked pastor looked to be choosing his words wisely. "I'm a chaplain."

"For real? You don't look like no preacher." Julio eyed the young man's tattoos, faded jeans, skull T-shirt and various piercings.

The man never broke eye contact with Vince. "I volunteer in the prison system."

Vince reacted as if a grenade had detonated in his pocket. His wordless mouth eased open and his eyes slid nearly shut, but not completely.

Val imagined Rowan's appearance made him approachable to inmates and was glad he had the guts to be who he was.

"Do you happen to be related to an inmate who was killed in the riot?"

Vince's face paled. He swallowed. Val reached sideways and grasped his hand. The teens didn't seem to notice Vince trembling as the two men stared at one another.

"Yeah. Victor Reardon."

"I spent a lot of time with him in the weeks prior to his death."

"Let's talk." Fiercely stoic, Vince motioned him toward the coffee lounge of the church.

"Hey, guys, let's go shoot some hoops," Brock said as he and Chance caught on to the conversation. They corralled the teens, veered them away from Vince and toward the gym.

"Thank you," Val mouthed, and followed Vince and the young chaplain.

Val stopped at the door, prepared to stay there and pace and pray for Vince.

But inside the doorway, Vince swiveled his head around as though frantically looking for something.

He always remained cool and collected under pressure. The turmoil in his face twisted her heart. She met his gaze, trying to infuse strength from afar.

He lifted his hand and waved toward the chair next to him.

Thank God, he was letting himself lean on her. Letting her in more and more.

Quietly, she joined the two men at a small round table. Vince reached for her hand. His palms were drenched.

She sent mental prayers upward for the conversation about to ensue. A blanket of peace descended. She tightened her grip, hoping Vince could feel God's peace, too.

"What can you tell me about my brother?"

"First of all, I wanna say that I'm sorry for your loss."

Vince nodded.

The chaplain cleared his throat. "I met him a few months before his death. Visited and prayed with him a few times before he started going to the prison church services. My band put on a rock concert for the inmates. Didn't preach or anything during the show, but we said we'd stick around for anyone who wanted to hang and talk about Jesus afterward. Your brother was one of those who stayed."

"Did you talk to him that night, too?" Vince's eyes glittered with tangible emotion.

"Yeah." The chaplain, voice thick, swallowed and maintained eye contact with Vince. "We talked with inmates who stayed after the show about how Jesus loved them and knew their situations."

"Did—did he listen to what you were sayin?"

"Unequivocally, yes. I personally prayed with him when he asked. Several of us prayed for and with the guys after the concerts."

"And you just happened to have been the one to seek out my brother?"

"*He* sought *me* out, actually. He was hungry for God, Vince. Trying to trust yet struggling to make sense of everything."

Vince's face turned a wounded kind of stormy. "Yeah, makes two of us."

"But I think he would have wanted you to know that a week or so later, he gave his life to Christ."

Vince's face fell into his hands, which he had disengaged from Val's.

Several moments passed where no one spoke. When Vince pulled his hands down, his eyes were clear but his palms were soaked. Val, feeling suddenly choked up for him, grasped his hand, mingling his tears in her hand.

"Can you tell me more?" Vince said in a raw voice.

"I kept in constant contact with him, as much as the prison would allow. Following his decision, he said for the first time since getting sent up that he didn't feel like he was losing his mind from the injustice of it all."

Vince blew out a breath. "He alluded to all this in a letter. I'm surprised it reached me overseas. He said he had something important to tell me but would wait until the next letter because it was complicated. But that he'd made a radical decision he wanted me to hear in detail and consider." Vince drew in a breath. "He died the next day."

"I'm sorry, bud."

Vince didn't seem to hear. "Are you certain he gave his life over to God before he died?"

"Yes. Without a doubt."

Relief whooshed out of Vince. He rested his eyes in his palms again but no tears fell this time. His broad shoulders rose with the deepest, purest breath she'd ever seen him take.

Maybe he hadn't wanted to believe in God because believing might have meant his brother's soul was lost.

Who knew Vince's reasoning? But clearly the issue of his brother's eternity was part of the darkness tormenting his soul. Part of the darkness from a troubled childhood, part of the pain she'd witnessed at the wreck yet was no longer present in his eyes.

"When I read the letter, I was pretty sure that's what it was. But I didn't want to hear that then. In my eyes he was befriending the enemy, meaning God and, no offense, but Christians."

Val giggled.

The chaplain eyed her curiously.

She rested her toe on Vince's foot and sought permission in his eyes to tell.

A cheeky grin altered his raw, stoic expression and he exerted gentle pressure back against her shoe.

"Vince is a proud member of Christianity now, by the way. Just recently."

The pastor's face lit. He grinned to a point that his face piercings moved. All four of them. "Congrats, man."

Vince shifted in his seat. "Before you go thinking I'm an ogre, I didn't discourage him because I thought that's the crutch he needed to get through being incarcerated for someone else's crime."

"Is that what you think now? That Christianity, or a relationship with Jesus, is a crutch?"

"No. Now I'm starting to think that my brother was the one who went behind bars and found freedom. And I'm the one who's been walking around locked in heavy shackles."

Chapter Twenty-One

"It's up." Vince carried the tray of hamburgers Val had grilled with great trepidation weeks later. She smiled nervously as people fixed their plates and began to dig in.

"It's good," Chance said.

Brock gave a thumbs-up and kept chewing.

"Wow, Vince, her burgers rival yours," Sarah said.

She figured that word had trickled out that Vince was trying to teach her to grill, and so people were just being nice. But hey, as long as none of them keeled over from food poisoning with her spatula as the murder weapon, things were all good.

The compliments continued as the teens, Vince's teammates and their loved ones feasted on her onion soup burgers.

As more compliments floated her way, Vince winked at Val and observed her with pride which trickled little thrills through her. She took her place next to him and crunched into her own juicy burger. "Actually, for once, I'm not feeling like I'm eating at my own risk."

Vince fisted his chest, nearly choking at that. He set his plate down and wrapped an arm around her shoulders, pulling her close. He planted a firm kiss on her head, before resuming his meal. "Good job, babe."

Friends around them grew quiet and Val felt their attention on her and caught curiosity dawning on faces around them. Doubt was dispelled about them dating.

For this was Vince's first public display of affection. And that affection was far from friendly but fell more in the realm of romantic.

When would he let the faith she knew to be growing like wildfire within him be known?

Knowing Vince, when he was good and ready.

Until then, she would not push. Just choose, as he had chosen to trust her profession as a prosecutor, that his profession of faith was real and right and true. He'd share in his own time.

"Finished?" Vince reached for her empty plate.

She handed it to him and he walked it over to the trash can alongside Aaron, who had Sarah's empty plate in hand as well.

"How's it going?" Sarah sidled up next to Val and asked, both their attention on their men.

"Really good."

"I hope everything works out."

"Me, too. So, are you excited for your wedding? Nervous?"

"Very. I wasn't nervous until I woke up yesterday and realized it's in two weeks."

"I'm excited for you."

"And I'm thinking news of another impending wedding isn't too far away." Sarah watched Val and grinned toward Vince. "Joel said the mission really turned him around as far as Christianity goes."

"That's what Vince said, too. So now I'm falling for him faster."

"Honey, you fell long ago. You're just falling out loud now."

"But that was a dangerous spot to be in. There were no guarantees that things could have gone this way." Which is why she hadn't let her heart truly engage until she was certain what Vince had with God was for real and forever.

Her guiding light had been God's exhortation to trust.

"So are you still thinking of a more serious future with him?"

"Yes, but I don't know if he's ready to settle down."

Sarah smiled. "We could get an idea."

Val straightened. "How?"

"Like after our wedding we could rig the garter and bouquet toss so that Vince will get the hint that you want him to propose, and see how he responds."

"Oh! I couldn't do that."

"Why not? Are you not ready? I don't want to rush things."

"Well, I am." Val and Sarah shared a secret laugh. "It's not that. I know he's the man for me. I know God ordained this union. It's just that I don't want us to overshadow you guys."

"Seriously, the way Aaron looks at it, we'd be honored. Aaron is the reason the team is in Refuge. He and Joel have prayed for their guys from day one. Vince helped Aaron through the loss of his first wife."

"I'd heard that. So, Aaron knows about this idea?"

"Yes. And he agreed. To be able to share the moment Vince realizes his dreams have come to fruition with regards to you, to have that happen at our wedding celebration would be so symbolic and mean so much to us."

"You're really not kidding."

"No. And Aaron feels the same way. Please? If you know you're ready and you know this is what you want, why wait to feel Vince out?"

"You're right. And it would catch him totally off guard." Val laughed. "Aaron knows you're over here trying to talk me into it, doesn't he?"

Sarah giggled. "Yes. Which is why he keeps getting in Vince's path and talking to him about nothing in particular every time he tries to skirt past him."

"If you are completely sure about this, then I'm game. What's the plan?"

"We'll save the garter and bouquet throwing until the end. I could intentionally walk the bouquet and pass it to you like a baton. And Aaron could do the same with the garter. Then once Vince began to question what was going on, you could do your lawyer thing and feel him out privately since the two of you are more of the private type."

Val nibbled her lip. "We might have to alert others about our plan. Do you think they'd keep it quiet?" After all, what if Vince looked appalled at the hint? Was this a good idea or one she'd live to regret?

"If Aaron threatened them with rucksack runs around the perimeter of Refuge Air Base if anyone lets it slip, yes."

Val drew a long breath and released it as possible scenarios and outcomes, both good and bad, chased one another through her mind. "I'll consider it. But don't hate me if I back out at the last minute or call our plan off."

"Okay." Sarah squeezed Val's hand. "Don't be afraid that it might chase him off. And I could never hate you."

Before they headed back from the side yard to the back, where Vince and Aaron were giving Aaron's preschool twins piggyback rides over the hill, Val grasped Sarah and gave her a sisterly hug. "You are a godsend. Your friendship is a tremendous blessing."

Tears filled Sarah's eyes. "I feel the same. I'm so glad Aaron knew me enough to know we'd be a good fit as best friends. And the impact you've made in

Vince's life—" Sarah swallowed hard. "We all care about Vince so much. Love the brooding bugger, even. But he could just not seem to accept that. Or God's love either. Until you came around."

Val giggled through a sudden onslaught of happy tears. "You mean until I crashed onto the scene."

Sarah laughed outright. "Hey, whatever it takes. That's what Aaron and Joel started praying for Vince.

"Whatever it takes," Sarah repeated as they started back around the house. "Now we just have to work on Chance and Brock and their devotion to God."

"By the way, none of the teenagers Vince and I host youth bashes for know how we met. I'd be embarrassed for them to know about the wreck."

Sarah snorted. "Then you probably told the wrong person. But, since we've become such good friends, I will *try* to hold your juicy secret in. Even though it'd be hilarious to tell what a terrible driver you are."

Val laughed and socked Sarah's arm. "You're honest at least. I know it'll be a struggle not to blab something so funny. But let's leave the blabbing to me. Vince is even sworn to secrecy."

Hearts locked in laughter and the joy of newfound friendship, they rounded the corner to discover controlled chaos in every corner of Aaron's yard. All-out fun. Everyone had dispersed to yard games or table activities after polishing off every single one of her burgers. A sense of accomplishment mingled with thankfulness for Vince's patient cooking lessons and the new passion for the Bible consuming him.

Vince, still toting one of the twins, bounced up making horsey noises. Little Bryce sent shrill laughs and squeals through the air as they circled her then stopped.

The image of Vince holding the little tyke awakened fierce longing for children of her own.

Of *their* own.

And this time she knew God was giving her the green light to dream of a future with this amazing man.

"What were you and Sarah up to?" Vince asked.

"What makes you think we're up to something?" Val stifled a grin and put on the poker face she used in court.

He eyed her as though he was looking for a blip on military radar. "Not sure. I guess it's completely normal for grown women to rush off giggling and cackling and whispering."

Val laughed. "We were planning something. But I'll let you in on it after their wedding."

"Does it have to do with the youth center?"

"What?"

"Aaron mentioned the old skating rink building's for sale. I figured Aaron told you we were thinking about renovating it. That's what he was yapping about over there when Sarah dragged you away."

"Yes, I recall a mention of it," Val hedged with all her heart. In truth, she'd overheard Aaron mention it to Sarah at the table. And he'd suggested Val check into it since the owner wasn't local and the building sat empty.

"Maybe we can see about reopening it. That'd be a new hangout place for the kids."

"Is it the one in my neighborhood?"

"Yeah. Aaron said there's a full apartment above it. Three bedrooms. Needs remodeling, but if someone didn't mind putting elbow grease into it, it could be a nice place to live."

"I could see about renting it out."

"Or you could see about living there since you'd talked about wanting to buy a house."

"We could see about going in together to get the building," she said tentatively.

"I'll run the youth center funding and you could fit the bill for the apartment side of it, which is the second story."

"That sounds like I'm getting the better deal with the least expense." She laughed.

"Whatever works. You spend time. I'll spend money." He grinned.

"I'll think about living there."

And moving you in as my husband after we get married if you respond positively to the hint and propose. She giggled.

He looked at her suspiciously again. "Happy today?"

"Yes. Very. I'm excited about what the future holds."

And happy that, because of God's blessing, it will hold us together. Hopefully. Doubt crept in like an unexpected crime witness.

His face sharpened in a way that let her know he

was intent on gathering more intel into why she was so giddy and alternately nervous.

If Miss Distraction was her name, then distraction would be her game.

She poked at the square shape in his shirt pocket. "What happened to the blue box?"

He grinned. "You can't stand to wait for surprises."

"No. And you can't stand not keeping me in suspense." She practically attacked his hand as it reached into his pocket and pulled out the box.

Rather than give it to her, he began to transfer it from one hand to the other and back again.

"Don't make me wait." She stomped on his toe.

"Consider it passive-aggressive payback."

Her cheeks colored at what that might mean, even though she knew he was kidding around with her. She loved that he could be forthright and funny all at the same time.

Anticipation rose as she followed the motions of his hands, rolling the box back and forth in his agile fingers. She grabbed at the box.

A small chuckle came out of him and he finally relented and opened the velvety hinged lid.

Just enough for her to glimpse tiny replicas. But she couldn't make out their shapes before he closed the box.

"More charms?" Giddiness rose within her.

"A few." He finally opened the box properly.

Her hands flew to her mouth and giggles slipped through her fingers. She reached for the three tiny pewter charms. Wait, not pewter this time. And he'd broken his call signature and given her four charms instead of three.

One tiny crystal cross.

One pewter replica of an open Bible.

One silver spatula.

One miniature gold ring.

Her heart pounded against her chest wall. She lifted the charms. "I know what the spatula and the little Bible symbolize. Our times together with Bible study and cooking classes."

He nodded, studying her with a tender, expectant expression but not offering the slightest hint of an explanation of the other two charms. Every charm he'd given her to date had something to do with the two of them, memories they'd made. Times and activities they'd shared together.

"So, I'm wondering if the cross and the ring are symbolic or literal or—"

"Both." He smiled.

She stifled a squeal.

He grinned. "I'm glad to see that you're finally catching on."

"The cross?"

"I've surrendered to it. To Him."

Her shriek filled the yard and caused several heads to turn. "For real?"

He nodded. "After the mission. I didn't tell you at first because I had to be sure."

"And you are?"

He nodded. "Never been more sure of anything."

She hurled herself into his arms and squished the stuffing out of him. "You have no idea how happy this makes me."

He coughed. "Can't. Breathe. Woman." He drew an exaggerated breath that she knew was nearly all drama. She couldn't squeeze the air from his large, muscular frame any more than she could squeeze it out of one of those grasshopper-like military helicopters they flew around Refuge on.

He peered down at her. "You act just like Joel did when I told him. Dude jumped in my lap. Man-hugs freak me out. But this—" his arms tightened around her "—I can definitely deal with."

She laughed. "He's probably exhilarated about your conversion. He's been praying for you a long time."

"Yeah, well now he and the guys can move on to their next victim." Laughing, he jerked a nod toward Brockton and Chance before turning back to Val. "But you can focus on me anytime you feel like it." He wiggled his eyebrows up and down then left his eyes flirtatiously hooded.

She recovered from the blush that secret sizzle in his eyes evoked. But not from the euphoria of knowing he was tucked safely inside a relationship with Jesus. She veered her gaze back to the last little charm. "I'm admittedly stumped about the little ring though."

"Are you? Because that one is different in that it

doesn't so much symbolize our past together, but what I hope to be our future. Consider it a promise of things to come. If you're game."

Her hands covered her mouth. "A promise ring?"

He nodded. "If you're, you know, down with that."

A promise ring! Promise rings came right before engagement rings!

That's it. All the encouragement she needed. She had to rig the hint at Petrowski's reception. Feel out her dark and brooding knight in black and chromed-out armor to see when she may be able to start looking forward to the real ring.

For now, she held out her wrist while he slipped the charms onto her bracelet. Hopefully Vince wouldn't take as long to promise to commit to her as he did to God. But, like God, she knew Vince was worth waiting for.

Her other bracelet, the one with four empty picture frames, the one Elsie had given her and the one she wanted to put her babies' pictures in, caught sunlight and seemed to beam a message.

And suddenly it came to her—exactly the words she would use to hint.

She giggled again. "I'm excited about Sarah and Aaron's wedding."

"Not me. There won't be a drop of booze." He scowled in mock distress.

She laughed. "Like you've been drinking."

"Who told you I stopped?"

"Pretty Boy."

He nodded facetiously. "Right. A little birdie."

"Are you nervous about going back to church tomorrow?"

"Was I nervous about going to church last week?" He tucked her hair behind her ear.

If he was, he hid it well. "I don't know. Were you?"

His expression turned deadpan. "Nope. Told you. Once I make up my mind about devoting to something, I'm all in and in for life."

His words paused her pulse and her steps. Anticipatory thrills rushed through her, because she knew he would apply those same principles of devotion to his relationship with Jesus, and to his union with her.

If he ever decided to propose.

Val eyed the former brooding bad boy.

Was he ready to settle down?

Two weeks from Tuesday would tell.

Chapter Twenty-Two

"**Y**ou ready for this?" Vince stood with his team in front of Petrowski at the decorated church on Tuesday.

"More than ready." Aaron peered through the crack in the door, where wedding guests were being seated in the sanctuary. "Wow, I think everyone in town came."

"We're all elated for you, bud. Good to see you happy again." Joel clapped a hand on Aaron's shoulder. Aaron had tragically lost his first wife to a drunk driver, and that sharp reminder recalled Aaron's world-tilting pain at that time and that hard season for their team. He'd had to make the hard choice of leaving pararescue for a time in order to care for his twin babies after their mother died. Joel, being the faithful leader and friend to Aaron that he was, had stepped up to fill both roles for a time. But Aaron was back in action.

Remembering Aaron's pain suddenly infused Vince with even more gratitude for God being in his life now. He hadn't realized until he'd stopped drinking recently just how close he'd come to following in his alcoholic father's footsteps.

Ben, guitar in hand, poked his head in. "Time to go."

The PJs offered knuckle bumps and soft *Oorah!*s as Aaron took his place near the young, tattooed pastor who'd prayed with Vince's brother. Vince hadn't realized until today that Aaron had asked Rowan to perform his and Sarah's ceremony. Maybe Rowan would perform his and Val's if she said yes to him when he proposed. He'd even had the marriage chat with Val's dad already.

The group—except for Joel, who was Aaron's best man, and Ben, who was to lead the singing during the service—slipped out from the room behind the stage and joined the other guests in the sanctuary.

Vince found Val, who had saved his seat. He sat next to her and kissed her on the cheek. "You look lovely."

Her mouth dropped open. "Nice compliment. No thug words."

"Not in church. Wait till we leave." Kidding, he laughed and grasped her hand as the wedding got under way.

All kinds of light, fluffy emotions rushed through him over the next half hour, emotions he had usually found unpleasant when being forced to observe someone's wedding. But not this time.

He could scarcely wait for the big day for Val and himself. Assuming she'd say yes.

Aaron and Sarah exchanged vows and Vince exchanged a shoulder bump and a meaningful look with Val, hoping she'd get the hint that he wanted them to be next.

She answered with a cheeky grin and a squeeze to his hand. And a bold, smug look? What was that all about?

Ben strummed his guitar and sang a song of worship. For the first time in his life, Vince gave himself to the song Ben sang to God. Aaron and Sarah had wanted all their friends and family to share in their first few moments of being man and wife by worshipping God and thanking Him for His goodness.

And for the first time in life, Vince could relate. As he let those first few awkward but heartfelt words of the song roll from his lips, tears slipped from Val's eyes, which seemed to assure him this awkwardness would get easier.

As she sang, she looked beyond radiant, the same way he felt right now. She let go of his hand to lift hers toward God and he followed her lead, knowing the focus shouldn't be on each other but God in these moments.

After Sarah and Aaron dismissed the guests, Vince led Val to the reception hall. Fun and laughter abounded as dances occurred and mishap was made by Aaron's adorable twins wreaking havoc and overdosing on sugar and mints at the punch and cake table.

"Let's go help Mina corral them." Val led Vince to assist Aaron's elderly housekeeper, who wasn't keeping up well with the rambunctious, sugar-coated boys.

Then came time for the last reception event, the garter and bouquet tosses. Aaron and Sarah got on the microphone together and asked everyone to line up for it.

Vince grinned at Val and shoved his single teammates away for the perfect spot.

He wanted that garter. But the other single guys looked just as intent on it.

Val skipped over and took her place next to the women. Who all stared at Vince with goofy grins. Odd.

Contrary to her normally competitive nature, Val slipped meekly to the back. Odder.

He tried to motion Val forward, so she'd be out in front and more likely to be able to catch the flowers as soon as Sarah flung them.

But Val slipped farther to the back instead. Behind the cluster of women. She seemed totally uninterested in catching anything airborne. She pulled out a file and zipped it leisurely across her nails instead. He waved his arms to catch her attention, but she never looked up.

Oddest. Frustration seeped in. Maybe he'd misread her interest.

Aaron and Sarah stepped down with garter and flowers in hand. Vince thought they were positioning themselves to toss the items, but while Aaron paused, Sarah kept walking.

What was going on? Something strange. What were they up to?

Vince looked around to see if anyone else thought their behavior odd. And realized that everybody in the entire place was staring at him. "What's happening?" Vince said to Brock and Chance beside him.

They just grinned but didn't answer. Vince met Val's gaze. She smiled but looked suddenly very nervous.

Something wasn't right. This felt too staged.

Vince eyed Aaron, who'd turned his back on the men, so he was getting ready to toss the garter.

It looked like Sarah was going to get closer to the girls. But she didn't stop at the edge of the horde of women.

She walked right into the middle of them.

The crowd parted like the Red Sea, and Sarah, smiling, walked calmly through the women, methodically, purposefully…

Directly to Val and placed the flowers in her hand.

Just then, Aaron whistled and raised his arms to toss the garter. Only, rather than rush to grab it, the men around Vince scrambled like fighter jets…away from him.

Stunned, Vince's arm snaked out…and he missed the catch. He bent to pick up the garter, perplexed because nobody, and he meant nobody—other than him—had tried to grab the thing.

Perplexed, Vince rose from picking up the garter to find Val walking toward him with the flowers. His heart began to beat faster at the looks his men gave him.

They were the same looks they'd given Aaron as he'd exchanged vows with Sarah a mere two hours ago.

Suddenly the focus was off Sarah and Aaron and totally on Vince and Val.

And he realized he'd been set up. One thing he told Val no one could accomplish. The realization that he'd been had made him laugh.

Suddenly, Val was upon him.

His hands began to sweat. His smile became gargantuan and his pulse rate grew exponentially while he tried to understand what this moment might mean. Brock clapped a hand on his back.

Vince eyed him. "You had to be in on this. You're the biggest practical joker I know."

Brock just grinned.

"And you, sneaky attorney that you are, how in the world did you manage to snow me?" Vince eyed Val and shook his head and went for a scary-sounding grumble but reached out his hand as she came near.

She laughed. "Come outside with me. I have another big surprise for you."

"Another?" He paused, not sure he wanted to continue. Especially since she looked as nervous as

Julio had when Vince caught him making out with a girl beside Val's fence one evening when she wasn't home. Vince knew all the good hiding places for stuff like that.

"There's someone you've been wanting to see for a long time." Val's eyes filled with joy.

Quite honestly stunned at what that could mean, Vince's teammates shoved him into motion.

Who was waiting outside for him?

Val led him into the open sunshine, hoping his sister, who'd arrived right before the wedding, knew when to make her appearance with Vince's refurbished bike.

Brock whistled what must have been a signal.

A Harley-sounding bike fired up around the side of the building. His sister, long black hair slicked back in a white-and-red bandana, rumbled on a sleek machine around the corner of the building.

Vince literally surged up on his toes at the sight of her. Victoria was the most welcome sight he'd ever seen. Victoria cut the engine and dismounted. The siblings both battled tears as slowly, wordlessly, they met and embraced. Val sniffed back tears along with most people around them as Victoria and Vince held each other, slightly swaying.

Victoria said something Val couldn't hear and Vince stepped back to eye the bike. He motioned his sister on it and mounted in front of her. Then, without saying goodbye to anyone, Vince took her for a ride.

Sarah approached Val. "He'll be back."

"I know."

But a half hour later, Val began to wonder. Pace. Fidget. "What's taking so long?"

"He'll be back," Sarah assured.

"What if he felt pressured or embarrassed with the hint?"

"Val, we're talking about Mr. Titanium here. Vince embarrassed? Never."

Chuckles sounded from folks mingling while they waited. But while they were right about Vince rarely being embarrassed, he was titanium-willed. If he felt pressed for action, he may resist.

"What if I misread him? What if he changed his mind?"

Sarah gave her a look. "What if you stop worrying and trust him?"

A rumble sounded from down the road. Val's nervousness fled. Until she saw Victoria returning on Vince's new bike—but no Vince.

Victoria dismounted, grinning, so Val determined not to fret. Seconds later a shiny new minibus, driven by a beaming Vince, pulled up in the church's carport where Val and the cluster of onlookers stood. Through tinted windows, Val saw passengers.

They remained on board while Vince got off the bus.

"A new van. Which church rented it to you?" She didn't know any churches in town with a van this nice.

"It's not rented. It's bought. Purchased by someone who plans to donate it to the church for youth events but who'll borrow it for youth bashes."

Val gasped. "You bought the van?"

Vince winked at the pierced pastor. "I had help. We did it to honor my brother. My teammates went in on it as well. Said they wanted me to save my cash for that skating rink you and I are reopening for Refuge."

Tears filled her eyes, followed by confusion as she saw the bus's passengers bustling about, scrambling and lowering and turning and…dressing? "Wait, what are they doing?"

Chuckling, Vince led her onto the bus so she could see for herself.

"Oh my word!" Val stared at the neighborhood kids in shock. Every teen had a safety helmet on and their torsos were covered in layers of bubble wrap. They all looked like little Michelin men.

Val blinked and shook her head, her mouth hanging wide open. "What on earth—?"

Vince laughed out loud, and behind her, the remaining wedding guests snickered.

Including Sarah. "Hey, I didn't tell."

Vince sent Val a grin that curled her toes and made her not care that every person in her neighborhood would now know she was the prosecutor who'd received a reckless driving citation.

Logan stood. "If we're gonna ride with you, we thought we'd better stick to the safe side and protect ourselves."

Val laughed out loud. "You finally told them how we met."

"No, but they they'll watch over the canned goods during the honeymoon."

She laughed outright, recalling how she and Vince and Aaron's PJ team had sneaked into his house and pranked it before the wedding.

She and Vince had personally helped Aaron's four-year-old twins peel off every label from the Petrowskis' canned goods. And Sarah must have stocked up. Val laughed again at the memory and its implications. "Oh, no, they won't. Wait! What honeymoon?" Aaron and Sarah's cans were already stripped.

Vince grinned. "I thought you'd never ask."

"Whaa—? Wait, if you didn't tell them about how we met, then who did?" Val's investigative skills kicked in as she studied the faces around her.

She blushed.

Vince smiled fondly at Victoria, whose eyes shone as she smiled up tentatively at the brother Val knew she loved. "A little birdie told them."

Val laughed. "A little birdie. Would that be the one that dive-bombs my head at Elsie's, or the one who builds motorbikes for a living and rivals you in the realm of stubborn and who I snuck clandestine phone calls to behind your back?" Val smiled lovingly at his sister as she said it. Victoria smirked and followed the crowd back inside.

Vince laughed. "I think you already know the answer to that. So I won't incriminate myself."

"Pleading the fifth, huh?" Vince pulled her close.

"Of course. So, on the case of the marriage proposal, kind sir, can I have your verdict please?"

"Yes, Your Honor. This way." He led her toward the youth bus. "When I left, you felt forgotten."

"Well, I was a little worried."

"And I was one step ahead." He guided her toward the back of the bus.

Vince came behind her in what she at first thought was a hug. But he covered her eyes with gentle hands and navigated her near what must be the back bus bumper.

Once paused, everyone had disbursed. His face reflected joy as vividly as Refuge's sun gleamed off the chrome on his new ride.

A message painted on the windshield, probably with a bar of soap, stood out against the sun-swathed glass.

Three words flanked by quotation marks formed the question that effused hope for the future and reflected the devotion of promise she'd been dreaming of for days. "Marry me, Val?"

He leaned his face for another kiss, which was when she heard the silence. She leaned back and looked around. They were alone. No one in sight. "Everyone left."

Vince held her tighter. "I asked them to."

"What? How? When?" Though admittedly, since she and Vince were wired to be more independent and private people, she was glad to share this intimate, priceless moment and the making of this memory solely with him. And God.

Vince laughed. "I had help. My bubble-wrapped minions spread out and let everyone know to get lost."

Val nodded, letting herself sway with Vince's gentle motion as he rocked back and forth with her still tucked firmly in his arms. "I'm glad that you had them ask people to let us do this alone."

He smiled. "So, Miss Distraction, what is the final verdict?" His gaze flitted to the question on the van. Hope twinkled like stars in eyes normally as dark and brooding as a starless night.

She pulled her hand up and played with the four empty squares on the pewter bracelet Elsie had given her. Then she met his gaze for an electric second. "Vince, I love you and would be honored to be yours always. And I can't think of anyone I'd rather have help me fill these lonely squares."

The biggest grin she'd ever seen spread across his face. "Always willing to oblige. You know how much I love adding to your collection. I'm charmed, pun intended." His claim-staking kiss sealed his words with the steel-bolted promise and hope for a marriage she knew would last through any hardship life had in store for them. Their love and God's would be their harbor.

Warmth spread across her hand as he lifted it close to his chest and slipped a sparkling diamond, encased in pewter, on her ring finger. "It's gorgeous!" she whispered, unable to stop staring at the facets or thanking God in her heart for winning Vince's and allowing her to do so as well.

"Not as gorgeous as you. Ride with me?"

Then he reached for her helmet and placed it on her head. They stepped over to the sleek new ride. Vince's face gleamed like the motorcycle's chrome as he swung his leg over the seat and held out his hand.

She placed hers in his and he tugged her toward the bike. His grin sent shivers from the tips of her fingers to the ends of her toes. Once she took her place near him, he donned his helmet and fired up the bike.

Power rumbled beneath her that matched the over-whelming sense of awe and thankfulness revving through her for God's goodness in pursuing her brooding PJ.

They pulled onto the road and the church sign across the street caught Val's eye.

New Beginnings.

She rested her cheek against her new fiancé's back and settled into contentment.

"Yes," she whispered, watching him as he expertly navigated his sister's gift down the street, increasing speed with more careful increments than he had the first few times she'd ridden with him.

"Yes," she whispered. "New Beginnings. Thank you, Jesus, for being more stubborn than the most stubborn man I know."

Vince tilted his head back and grinned. Then revved the bike and leaned into her embrace as her arms wrapped tighter around him, reveling in their new beginning as an engaged couple.

Bliss.

* * * * *

Dear Reader,

Vince has been the bad boy of the pararescue team in my Wings of Refuge series. His story was so fun to write because we finally get to see him redeemed. The romance aspect of this story was challenging because Vince wasn't a Christian in the beginning of the book. I receive a lot of letters from young people, and I didn't want to give off the impression that it's okay to fall for someone who doesn't share our faith. If you have children, I hope you pray for them and their future mates. I came to God because people prayed for me. If you are single and still looking, I hope you will obey God's precepts and let Him lead you as Val did.

Look for the next PJ story in spring 2010, wherever books are sold.

I love hearing from readers and would especially love feedback on discussion questions regarding future books and characters. E-mail me at: cheryl@cherylwyatt.com or write me at P.O. Box 2955, Carbondale, IL 62902-2955.

If you'd like new-release news and goodies only available to my quarterly newsletter subscribers, visit my Web site at www.cherylwyatt.com and sign up in the space provided. I respect your privacy and will not share your information with a third party.

Thank you for spending time with me in fictional Refuge. Your readership is a tremendous blessing.

Cheryl Wyatt

QUESTIONS FOR DISCUSSION

1. Did you understand and/or agree with Val's reasons for moving to a downscale neighborhood? Why or why not?

2. Do you think Val was in a dangerous place with her emotions before she knew for certain Vince would come to God? Please discuss.

3. Why do you think Vince and Val were so attracted to one another? Could it have been a case of opposites attract at first?

4. What do you imagine Vince and his formerly estranged sister, Victoria, said to each other near the end of the book?

5. Between Brock and Chance, which teammate do you think is closer to devoting themselves to God and why?

6. If you could choose a youth theme for the new skating rink, what would you choose and why?

7. How do you think Val would have responded had Vince never devoted himself to God? Would she have rejected him? Accepted his proposal?

8. Do you think Elsie gave Val sound advice regarding Vince? Why or why not?

9. The teens were drawn to Val and Vince because the adults spent time getting to know them. Was there anyone like that in your life when you were an adolescent? How did that affect your decisions?

10. If Vince hadn't devoted himself to God after meeting Val, having the wreck and having his mission go awry, what do you think it would have taken for him to do so?

11. Do you know someone like Vince who is hostile toward God? Are you willing to pray "whatever it takes"?

12. Do you think it was God's goodness and unwavering devotion that drew Vince? Or the struggles that came his way? Please discuss.

Scandal surrounds Rebecca Gunderson after she shares a storm cellar during a deadly tornado with Pete Benjamin. No one believes the time she spent with him was totally innocent. Can Pete protect her reputation?

Read on for a sneak peek of HEARTLAND WEDDING *by Renee Ryan, Book 2 in the* AFTER THE STORM: THE FOUNDING YEARS *series available February 2010 from Love Inspired Historical.*

"Marry me," Pete demanded, realizing his mistake as the words left his mouth. He hadn't asked her. He'd told her.

He tried to rectify his insensitive act but Rebecca was already speaking over him. "Why are you willing to spend the rest of your life married to a woman you hardly know?"

"Because it's the right thing to do," he said.

Angling her head, she caught her bottom lip between her teeth and then did something utterly remarkable. She smoothed her fingertips across his forehead. "As sweet as I think your gesture is, you don't have to save me."

A pleasant warmth settled over him at her touch, leaving him oddly disoriented. "Yes, I do."

She dropped her hand to her side. "I don't mind what others say about me. You and I, *we,* know the truth."

Pete caught her hand in his, and turned it over in his palm. "I told Matilda Johnson we were getting married."

She snatched her hand free. "You…you…*what?"*

He spoke more slowly this time. "I told her we were getting married."

She did *not* like his answer. That much was made clear by her scowl. "You shouldn't have done that."

"She was blaming you for luring me into my own storm cellar."

The color leached out of Rebecca's cheeks as she sank into a nearby chair. "I…I simply don't know what to say."

"Say yes. Mrs. Johnson is a bully. Our marriage will silence her. I'll speak with the pastor today and—"

"No."

"—schedule the ceremony at once." His words came to a halt. "What did you say?"

"I said, no." She rose cautiously, her palms flat on her thighs as though to brace herself. "I won't marry you."

"You're turning me down? After everything that's happened today?"

"No. I mean, *yes.* I'm turning you down."

"Your reputation—"

"Is my concern, not yours."

She sniffed, rather loudly, but she didn't give in to

her emotions. Oh, she blinked. And blinked. And *blinked.* But no tears spilled from her eyes.

Pete pulled in a hard breath. He'd never been more baffled by a woman. "We were both in my storm cellar," he reminded her through a painfully tight jaw. "That means we share the burden of the consequences equally."

Blink, blink, blink. "My decision is final."

"So is mine. We'll be married by the end of the day."

Her breathing quickened to short, hard pants. And then…*at last*…it happened. One lone tear slipped from her eye.

"Rebecca, please," he whispered, knowing his soft manner came too late.

"No." She wrapped her dignity around her like a coat of iron-clad armor. "We have nothing more to say to each other."

Just as another tear plopped onto the toe of her shoe, she turned and rushed out of the kitchen.

Stunned, Pete stared at the empty space she'd occupied. "That," he said to himself, "could have gone better."

* * * * *

*Will Pete be able to change Rebecca's mind
and salvage her reputation?
Find out in HEARTLAND WEDDING
available in February 2010
only from Love Inspired Historical.*

Love Inspired® SUSPENSE

RIVETING INSPIRATIONAL ROMANCE

Watch for our new series of
edge-of-your-seat suspense novels.
These contemporary tales
of intrigue and romance
feature Christian characters
facing challenges to their faith...
and their lives!

NOW AVAILABLE IN REGULAR
& LARGER-PRINT FORMATS

Steeple
Hill®

Visit:
www.SteepleHill.com